HUNTER

By
Bobby Sanders
Copyright 2016

If no one reads this but me, it will have been worth it.

I dedicate this work to my Father, Don Sanders and My Grandfather, Grant Sanders. The sayings and the humor came from them. The characters in this work are fictional some of them have the names of people that I know, even some of their personalities are the same. The work is fictional if you read your name in here it's because I like you and you were on my mind.

Table of Contents

Chapter 1 – Alone with His Tools

Solitude... Seemed like everywhere he went he was alone. It was alright though. He liked it that way. Solitude had a way of letting a man know his own mind. All his thoughts were his own, not seeds planted by listening to someone else's useless opinion. Here he was, alone with his thoughts again. About a hundred miles north of the Texas line in the Indian Nations, camped on a sand bar on the Washita River. Him, his thoughts, his horse, and a wanted poster he'd pulled from the Sheriff's office wall in Wichita Falls. His name was Frank Hunter. Funny how the name fit they'd say when he collected the rewards. Hunter never saw anything funny about it. It was a dirty job, but it paid well enough.

He'd picked up a lead along the Red River from a dirt farmer who said he'd seen the guy in the drawing six days ago. Allowed how he was headed to Colorado, or was it Ft. Smith, he couldn't recall. Maybe a silver dollar would help him remember.

Hunter allowed he'd recall the broken thumb long after he forgot the guy's destination. Turned out he remembered just fine.

Ft. Smith was two hundred miles away still. A week on horseback if the weather held. This time of year it rarely did.

A small band of reservation Chickasaws hunting whitetails crossed the river about a half mile downstream. They gave Hunter a look for a minute and went their way. Frank finished his coffee and started to pack up for the day. Arkansas wasn't getting any closer, and he didn't want those six young bucks to have enough time to get the guts up to try to take his horse and rifle. They called them the civilized tribes here, but he'd seen how uncivilized they could be when they had the numbers.

As he packed he counted the things he kept on the trail. Remarkable how few one really needs. Coffee pot; gotta have that. Coffee he kept in a little buckskin drawstring bag. He needed to restock next trader or general store he saw. One small cast iron skillet, about nine inches in diameter. It served as cooking pot for the scrawny rabbit that was supper last night and dinner plate. Salt, pepper, bedroll, and the canvas pouch where he kept the supplies he used to clean his tools. They all fit in the saddle bags except the bedroll, which tied onto the back of the saddle he'd brought home with him from the War. Then there were his tools.

His tools consisted of a good handmade Bowie Knife about 14 inches long, brass pommel, bone handled, sturdy a knife as he'd ever seen. He'd won it in a card game off a buffalo hunter in Garden City, Kansas last summer. Guy was a good loser. Frank had bet ten dollars against that knife, won it with a pair of jacks.

Next in the tool kit was a little Sheriff's Model Colt tucked into the pocket sewed inside the sleeve of his coat. An Army Colt hung at his right hip on a belt with .44 caliber shells stuffed into the loops haphazardly. He had two boxes of .44-40 ammo in his saddle bag but didn't want people to think him that well outfitted. On his left side was the Smith and Wesson Schofield he'd kept from a bank robber he'd trailed to Kansas last summer. He wore it cross draw style. On the saddle were a Winchester 1873 and a Greener sawed off double 12 gauge. All used the .44-40 except the shotgun and the Schofield. Damned odd ball, he'd trade it for a good Colt next time he had the chance.

He mounted up and headed east across the Washita and across the plains. This part of the Territory was littered with creeks and streams so water wasn't really a concern. Other places it had been- the Kansas prairie, where the dry brown grass stretched on for days, or West Texas, out south of Amarillo. In the summer the creeks dry up and everything dies till spring, not here though. In the West center of the Indian Territory it was wet and green this spring of 1885. He had one canteen filled though he didn't need it. He rode east and thought his thoughts.

Chapter 2 – Evening Visitor and the Boy

David Lowe was the name on the poster from Wichita Falls.

He'd robbed the bank in Decatur, Texas on April Fool's Day, killed the town constable and lit out for the Territories. The County Sheriff wouldn't come into the Nations after him, and the Famous Texas Rangers had their hands full further west and south with raiding Mexican bandits, and Geronimo's last band of Apaches. So they let him run and printed posters, knowing Hunter or someone like him would come along and hunt him down for five hundred dollars, dead or alive.

Five hundred dollars was a fair amount in those days when a good horse could be bought for fifty bucks, another twenty five for a saddle and tack. Five hundred could outfit Hunter for a year if he was frugal, and he was. He was also greedy. Frank had a woman in Texarkana. Saloon girl back when she was a girl. She ran the girls at the Three Doors Saloon now. When business was slow she'd sit on the piano and sing to the drunks and cowboys. They'd tip her for singing and she'd occasionally go upstairs with one if she felt like it. She didn't have to though. Frank Hunter sent her half of all the bounties he collected.... old debt... and when Hunter came home to Texarkana, Marla was all his.

While Hunter was twisting that farmer's thumb he told him Lowe had come through and camped on the river and shared coffee and beans with him. Told of how he had enough cash to set him up a livery in Arkansas. He was headed home to do just that. Gonna be a business owner and marry a good woman.

Frank remembered thinking she'd be a young, red eyed, livery sellin', widow next week if ol' Dave didn't dally too long in the Territories. Maybe Frank would let him get close enough to smell the dream before he put the tools to work. "Dead or alive" meant dead to Hunter. He didn't want to talk.

The next night Hunter camped outside a small settlement on the South Canadian. He'd bought coffee and a pint of good bourbon whiskey. A pint lasted Frank a week or more usually. As a rule Frank didn't drink to excess. He knew what he was capable of when he was in the bottle. A mean drunk with talented hands was Frank Hunter. Marla had warned him about it several times and he believed her. He sipped a little sip and stared into the fire.

He heard the twig break when the horse thief was still 40 yards away. As the vagrant drifter approached Hunters fire he heard him cock both barrels of a shotgun. Frank raised his hands and asked "What's this friend?"

The drifter replied "Well mister I'm tired of walkin' so I figure it's your turn to walk a while. I'll take them pistols."

Franks rifle and shotgun were leaned against a tree close to his bedroll away from the fire. Frank carefully dropped the Army Colt and the Schofield on the soft grass near the edge of the clearing and put his hands on his head. The drifter walked past him admiring the fine horse he'd just procured when Frank's right hand crept into the left sleeve of his coat, finding the Sheriff's Colt there. He shot the horse thief in the right ear at a range of about two feet. The right ear bled a little. The left side of the drifters head blew off in a bony spray that covered the bushes at the edge of the camp. Hunter ejected the spent casing and reloaded one of the two empty chambers careful to leave the one left empty under the hammer. Frank sat back down and sighed. Someone always had to fuck up something, didn't they?

Next morning Hunter covered the body of his evening guest with some stones from the river bank right where he fell. He now had an extra shotgun and 6 more twelve gauge shells than he had last night. He'd sell the shotgun in Webber's Falls. He smiled to himself and thought, "Makin' money while sittin' on my ass drinking bourbon. Don't get much easier than that." He had no idea that he'd give that shotgun away in a couple of days, along with half of his 12 gauge ammo. He saddled up, stowed his gear and rode east along the river a ways.

Around noon he crossed the river at a little narrow spot and met two old Indians sitting in the shade. They were about half way down a jug of cheap corn mash whiskey and very

friendly. Frank understood about half of their lingo and the rest
he made out by their hand gestures.

The older one of the two had an old rusty single shot
shotgun but no shells. Since they were too old to pull a bow (and
too drunk) they hadn't eaten in three days. Frank gave them two
shells. He wouldn't let a dog starve, let alone two happy drunks.
He asked how long the two had been camped there along the
river.

The younger one said. "Twelve suns".

Frank pulled out the wanted poster and showed them
Lowe's picture. They both started at the sight. After much
jabbering Hunter couldn't make out, he learned that Lowe had
camped with them 5 nights ago and he had helped them finish
off the jug before this one. While he was drunk he had showed
them a bag of money. Said he was a rich man. He had been gone
in the morning with the last of their deer jerky. They didn't care
for the money but Lowe had stolen a weeks food from them.

They asked Frank to kill the thief for them if he caught him.

Hunter told them they could count on it.

Suddenly the younger of the two grabbed the old single
shot and stuffed one of Franks two shells in it. Hunter's hand
went to the butt of the Schofield. The old man was on his left side
and cross draw would bring the muzzle to bear faster. He pulled
up and shot an old gray 'possum. He nodded at his camp-mate
and said nothing. Frank knew that was two nights stew for them.
Franks stomach rumbled, sometimes 'possum was damned good
if it was hot. He'd look for a rabbit or a turkey this evening. He
rarely had anything to eat other than supper. Coffee in the
morning was about his diet.

Frank headed east and left his two new friends skinnin'
'possum. He'd already talked today more than the last week
combined. He was ready to be alone again. A big dark cloud was
brewing in the Southwest. Frank had seen these before. In the
nations a storm could bloom up out of nowhere, rain and hail to

beat the band, sometimes they'd put down a cyclone or two, then they'd just be gone, and the sun would shine like it never happened. This looked like one of those clouds. Dark with a lot of lightning and a big mushroom shaped top on it. It was headed this way fast.

Hunter rode up the nearest hill to look for some cover and lucked out. About four hundred yards north was an abandoned sod house cut into the side of the hill. He headed there at a gallop. When he was close enough Hunter yelled "Hello the House". When he got no reply, he dismounted and went in. It was sturdy enough- cut sod walls a foot thick. There was a big hole in the roof. It looked like there had been a stove in the corner, but whoever had built the house took the stove when they left, took the front door too. Left the strap hinges though. Frank led his horse in and unsaddled him. Probably be here a while. Put his two shotguns and his rifle in the corner furthest from the door and the hole in the roof. They'd stand a dousing and had many times, but why clean and oil them if you didn't have to.

Frank went about making sure his bedroll and coffee were in a dry place along with his saddle. He looked out at the clouds and his stomach rumbled again

Hunter grabbed the Greener from the corner, unlatched the breech and made sure the scatter gun was loaded. Maybe he could find a rabbit before the storm set in. He didn't. He saw another 'possum but didn't have the makings for a stew and fried 'possum was nasty as hell. It started to spit a little rain. He headed back to the sod house in a hurry. It was fairly pourin' when he made it in the open door; as he was shakin' the rainwater out of his hat he caught the movement out of the corner of his eye. Years of living in the wild lands like this had trained Hunter's hands to work even before his mind knew what they were doing. The hammers were back on the Greener and the twin barrels were pinned against the boy's chest before Hunter even knew it was a boy. His first two fingers already had pressure on the twin triggers. He eased the pressure up but didn't move the scatter gun's muzzle.

"What you think you're doin' here, boy?" Hunter barked at the shivering kid.

"I'm Ju-ju-just tryin' to get dry mister." Came back in a whimper. "Don't shoot me pu-pu-please."

Frank looked down at the Greener. He lowered the muzzle then lowered the hammers carefully. He looked the boy up and down in silence for a full minute. He was a tall thin boy, tow headed with a dimple in his chin. He looked strong under the home-made coat that Frank was sure his momma had made for his daddy. It didn't fit him right. He was gaunt and leathery and the thinness he had seen at first was the result of malnutrition. He was a big kid and if he'd been fed would've weighed in about one hundred eighty pounds Frank judged. In his current state he'd be surprised if he topped one-forty soakin' wet, which he was. The kid was probably 16 years old. "Body of a man, mind of a boy, still longin' for his momma's tit." Hunter thought.

Frank said, "Have that wet coat off and hang it on the peg, it's gonna rain a while." Just then the first close thunderclap hit and the boy winced away from the sound. Frank noticed the terror in his eyes. Terror was something Hunter knew when he saw it. He'd seen it countless times in the eyes of the men he tracked... and in mirrors.

The boy hung up the coat to dry and looked at Frank through his uncut blonde hair. Frank said, "You look half starved son. How long since you ate something?"

The kid said, "Four days sir."

"Don't call me sir. Hunter's my name. What's yours?"

"Donnie" The boy said.

"Well Donnie after this storm passes we'll hunt us up something to eat before you pass out." They waited in silence for the rain to stop. Frank still holdin' the Greener across his lap and the boy, Donnie, waitin' to see if this big man was gonna use it.

After the rain stopped the woods along the river smelled

sweet with the spring rain and wet grass. Hunter walked slow and easy with the shotgun on his shoulder. The kid was on the other side of the thicket trying to chase anything out Frank's way. They had two fat cottontails and two quail in a half hour. Frank thought huntin' was a lot easier with a helper. They went back to the sod house and built a fire. The dead fall was wet but there was enough dry kindling in the house, along with two old boards and a broken table leg. He got a good flame going then added some of the wet wood. It dried out quickly and soon the smell of rabbit frying filled the air. The boy ate all the first rabbit Frank fried and both the quail. Frank slowly ate the other rabbit while the coffee brewed. After he had his coffee cup full and settled in against the side of the sod house he asked, "What are you doin' out here in the Territories alone and starvin', boy?" The boy stared into the guttering fire. He was dry warm and full for the first time in what seemed like years. He was big but only a boy and the tears betrayed that fact. He wiped them away with his sleeve and started in on the story he had to tell to the man who had saved his life.

"My name is Donnie. I don't have a last name, at least not that I know. I have lived as a worker for a man in Arkansas who traded with the Tribes. He told me my Ma and Pa traded me for a mule and supplies when I was five. I kinda remember Ma. Anyway I been workin' for this man who traded for blankets, whiskey, old wore out rifles, anything the redskins would buy or trade for. I loaded the wagon, and set up the tradin' table. The trader's name was Preston. He would beat me if I knocked over a whiskey keg or dropped something. He'd not let me eat if I did anything he didn't like. It went on that way all my life, Mister. Then five nights ago we were camped about twenty miles north of here at a little Indian settlement. Business was closed for the day and I was washin' the pots from supper when I heard a sound from the bushes. I went to look and it was old Preston on top of an Indian girl. She was no more'n ten or twelve years old. I hit him in the back of the head with the camp shovel. He was still breathin' so I told the girl to run. She did and so did I. I ran all night and half the next day before I stopped to rest. Even then I hid in a plumb thicket. I been walkin' south ever since. Mr. Hunter you're the first person I seen since that Indian girl ran away."

The tears had cut clean tracks in the dirt on his face but, Frank could tell he felt better havin' it off his chest. Frank said, "Get some sleep, Kid, you're safe tonight". That was how it started.

Chapter 3 – Rememberin'

Hunter didn't sleep much that night. The similarities between Donnie's story and his own were remarkable. He hadn't thought about some of it in years. He guessed the mind didn't bring back the things that hurt (on purpose). Frank had lived at home, but the abuser had been his Pop. Pop liked to beat Frank's Momma when the wash hung on the line too long, or if the beans and bacon were too salty, or just if he felt mean.

Frank caught his share of the beatin's too, but nothing like Momma did. One night Momma had stopped Pop from getting over on Frank's nine year old sister Liz. She earned a beating for her trouble. Pop left Momma in the barn crying and bleeding. Frank hit Pop in the head with the ax from the wood box. He went down without a sound. Hunter remembered thinking, "Damn that was easy, should have done it a long time ago." Momma was sad because deep down she still loved Pop, but she was glad to see him gone too.

Frank left the next morning. Momma packed him a change of clothes, bread and cheese enough for three days, and a canteen full of well water. He never saw his Momma again. Frank enlisted in the Confederate army, lied and said he was seventeen. He was fifteen years old in the fall of '61. The army fed him and clothed him and taught him a trade for the next four years. He'd learned on his own that killin' was easy. They taught him to do it well.

On the day Frank left home he walked south. No particular reason it's just the way the road went. He kept going seemed like weeks but when he reached Shreveport he still had a little cheese left so it must have been three or four days. He missed Momma something awful. Like young Donnie his tear tracks were clean and white on his dirty face. He got into Shreveport and started looking for work. No one was hiring.

A cook at the back door of a café gave Frank a corned beef sandwich. It was fine. The cook told him on the east side of town Major Wheat was camped out there raising a battalion of men to go fight the Yankees, called themselves the Lousiana Tigers.

Frank thought "What the hell, at least he wouldn't starve." He walked east.

When he got there a surly Sergeant with an Irish accent told him "We ain't takin' no babies, Laddy."

"I ain't no baby." Frank met his stare defiantly.

The sergeant must've like his salt because after a minute he said "Come with me Laddy." He took him to the front of the line and gave him to Lt. Thibodaux. He said "Lieutenant, here's a boy who wants to die for the Confederacy."

Lt. Thibodaux looked at Frank Hunter a while and said "That true Kid?"

Frank looked back at the Lieutenant and said. "No sir, I just wanna kill Yankees."

They signed him up on the spot. Over the next four years he killed more than his share of Yankees. They trained him at Ft. Monroe in Louisiana. Then they shipped him by train to West Virginia. They gave him a fine Sharps Rifle and put him to work.

By the time the Lousiana Tigersdisbanded in late '62 Frank had thirty five notches cut in the stock of that Sharps. He had another five notches cut in the butt of the old Colt's Dragoon he'd taken off a dead blue-belly Captain. He'd also taken his saber, but had traded it for some boots.

He fought with several outfits after Major Wheat got it and

the Tigers split up. He had a knack for this kind of work. It suited him. He wasn't a bad person, he was just suited for killin'.

When the war was over, Frank mustered out in Nashville. He sold a few war souvenirs and bought a decent roan mare and a saddle; the same saddle he rode now. He still had hard tack and ammo for the pistol, he wouldn't starve. He headed west for home.

He got to Texarkana on a fine late October afternoon. He went straight to the house he grew up in; he found it deserted with pigeons roosting and shitting on Momma's dining room floor. He looked out by the barn and found the grave. It was next to Pop's with a white wooden plank that just read "Augustine Hunter...died sick".

Frank asked the neighbors down the road. They weren't friends, just acquaintances. They didn't know what happened or where Liz was. She would be fourteen now. With Momma gone and no kin close by she could be anywhere.

Frank Hunter was twenty years old now, almost twenty-one. He left the house that was his now. He went back into town and walked into the old Three Door Saloon and ordered a bottle and a glass. He laid down one of three U.S. dollars he had and started drinking.

Three men playing cards across the room started talkin' loud about how the Confederate army must've laid down for ol' U.S. Grant at Appomattox. This rubbed Hunter the wrong way, but he kept silent. He wanted no trouble. They said how Lee just wanted to go home and sold the South out. Hell, Lincoln was dead we had 'em licked. Then one of 'em said something about the Lousiana Tigers and how they couldn't fight their way out of a cat house. Frank turned up the bottle and drained the last two inches of cheap sour mash, stood up and broke the bottle across the man's nose obliterating his face. Shards of glass were embedded in one eye and both cheeks. His tough talking friends shrank back as Hunter pulled the big dragoon.

Suddenly she was there, beautiful and innocent looking, but

with an air that said she was anything but. She stood right in front of the barrel of the big revolver and said "Put that away now." Taken aback by the beauty of the girl and the idiocy of her actions, Frank put the Colt's Dragoon back in the holster. She sat Frank back down at a table and got ol' Mr. Shredded Face's friends to take him down the street to the Doc's office, and then she sat down.

She said "Marla Anderson's my name. What's yours?"

"Frank Hunter." He replied still kinda shocked and more than a little drunk.

"Men who are capable of doin' that kind of thing shouldn't drink, Frank. It'd be too easy for you to have killed all three of those loud-mouths, even Three Sheets to the Wind like you are. You would've too, Frank, I saw it in your eyes."

Chapter 4 – The question

The boy stirred in his sleep. It brought Hunter out of his thoughts. He hadn't thought about the war in a while. It was a terrible thing for a country to tear itself apart like it did. Even now twenty years later there were strong feelings on both sides... especially the South.

Hunter lay down and finally slept. He had to get back on the trail early if he wanted to catch Lowe while he was still in the Territories. He dreamed of War, and Momma, and Marla.

The sun rarely got up and caught Frank Hunter sleeping but this morning it did. He opened one Eye and there was Donnie looking at him.

Donnie said, "You had some awful dreams Mr. Hunter."

Frank Said, "Hunter... not Mr. Hunter. I ain't Mr. anything."

"Ok... Hunter. You talked real mean and loud in your sleep." Frank poured water from the canteen to start some coffee. He was stirring the coals from last night's fire when the kid asked him the question Hunter knew was coming.

"Can I ride with you Hunter? I got nowhere else to go."

You could feel the silence as the boy who reminded Hunter so much of himself at that age waited for an answer.

"I don't have another horse for you to ride. How you gonna ride with me? And I don't need another mouth to feed. (Frank remembered the hunt last night being so easy with a flusher). I don't like talking to folks that's all. I like it alone just fine."

Donnie waited for Hunter to finish before he said anything, lettin' him soak it up at his own pace. He'd learned to work ol' Preston the same way. Plant an idea and let it grow till Preston thought he'd come up with it on his own.

After Frank had a few minutes to think on it Donnie said "I don't eat much." He left it at that for a minute. Then "You don't have to talk to me." A couple more minutes then; "I could help you."

Hunter looked flatly at the boy and said "Help Me? You don't even know what I do."

Donnie answered "I guessed you were an outlaw of some kind."

"You guessed close. "Hunter said. "Just the other way around. I'm a bounty hunter." The kid smiled.

Frank said "Don't even think about sayin' it".

Donnie said "It's just kinda funny a bounty hunter named Hunter." Hunter looked at him and the kid shut his yap. Hunter's eyes weren't smiling and he could see the anger in there.

Hunter went on. "Like I said you didn't miss it much. I have to think and act, like an outlaw. I have to out shoot, out think, out ride, and out kill them or they'll kill me. I only take the ones wanted dead or alive. Dead is so much quieter on the trip in. I go where I want, track who I want. When I have enough cash I go home for a while. When the cash gets low there's always a wanted poster at the sheriff's office. I make out alright. It's a one man job, Kid. I don't need a partner."

Donnie asked "Can I tag along to the next settlement at least?"

Hunter said. "If you can be quiet." They drank coffee,

Hunter from the one cup, Donny from the skillet.

The kid could be quiet... For about 2 minutes at a time. Questions like. "Who was the meanest outlaw he'd ever went up against?" And who had the Fastest Draw?" And the one Hunter knew was coming. "How many men had Hunter killed?" Hunter said flatly one hundred seventeen. Donnie went silent. Even though he was behind Hunter riding double up on the horse he could tell the kids jaw dropped open. "Of course sixty eight of those were in the war, thirty eight for bounties in the past nineteen years. Then there was Pop."

The kid asked "You killed your own father?"

"Yup."

After a moment the boy said "Why"?

Hunter, knowing the kid couldn't see his grin said. "Talked too much."

Donnie said three more words the rest of the day.

They camped that night outside a settlement in the hills. Two wagon roads crossed and there was a creek. That's all you need for a town to spring up. Indians, people who sell to the Indians, people who buy from the Indians. Frank told the boy to start the coffee. The kid was doing a fair job of building a fire when frank left. He left the extra shotgun there in case the kid needed it.

Frank got to the livery and looked around for the owner. He found him in the back warming up a can of beans. "You got any horses for sale mister?"

"In fact I do." Came the cheerful answer. "Those two in the front two stalls." He kept on stirring his beans while Hunter had a look. One was a sway backed old mare that looked like a fifteen year old pack horse, carried too many pounds too many miles. The other though. It was a two year old paint filly, good lines, shod and a long mane to grab when the trail got rocky.

The hostler came in and asked. "Well what'cha think?"

Hunter said the paint was a good lookin' animal but the mare would make fine glue. The hostler laughed his agreement.

"I need a saddle too, nothin' fancy."

He said. "Got this old thing I'll throw in if you buy that paint."

"What'cha askin' for her?"

"Take Fifty dollars for the horse and saddle. You ride her away." Just then the paint turned and tried to bite Hunters shoulder.

The liveryman flushed at Hunters stare and said. "Forty."

Hunter took off his hat and turned down the band and took out two twenty dollar gold pieces and said. "You saddle her."

He got back to camp and told Donnie he wouldn't be afoot anymore. Donnie looked at the paint pony like she wasn't real. Hunter said, "Un-saddle her and take that bit out and we'll tie 'em out over there in the grass for the night."

The kid's eyes expressed what he didn't have words to say. No one had ever treated him better or cared for him more than this killer of men who wanted him to just shut up. He hoped against hope that Hunter wouldn't make him leave in the morning. They shot two squirrels, they cooked up fine.

After the hunt Frank said. "You may as well keep that old scatter gun. I got two."

Donnie said. "I better not Hunter. I don't know how I'm gonna pay you back for the horse, let alone a shotgun too."

Hunter replied. "Who said anything about payin' me back? I give them things to you to help you get a start. Sometimes a start is all a fella m needs."

They cleaned the shotguns in silence. "Gotta take care of the tools…" Hunter preached… "Before anything. If your horse dies you can survive out here but without a gun you can't". After they finished Hunter rummaged in his saddlebags and came out with fourteen twelve gauge shells. He gave seven of them to Donnie and said. "Load it up. Without shells it's a hammer." Donnie loaded the old scatter gun and leaned it against a tree.

Donnie laid down and rested his head on his new saddle. He was the happiest he had ever been, but he was still apprehensive. He couldn't tell what Hunter wanted him to do. Ride along, or get lost. He slept though, and dreamed of ridin' the trail with Hunter, trackin' some killer from Texas. Hunter on his big brown gelding, him on his paint filly, such adventures they'd have.

Hunter laid down as well. He had a decision to make and needed to make it now. The trail was getting colder by the minute and he needed to be gone early tomorrow. First he'd show the poster around the settlement then head out after Lowe. It took Frank about two minutes to make up his mind, then he slept. No dreams tonight, funny how resolution can do that for a man.

Chapter 5 – Partnered Up

The sun didn't catch Frank Hunter sleeping this morning. The smell of coffee was already in the air when the first rays peeked through the trees. Hunter walked over and kicked the boy's foot. "You gonna sleep all day?" He barked. Donnie was up in a flash, getting his boots on. Hunter said "Set yourself down on that rock we need to talk." He could see the disappointment in Donnie's eyes as he dragged over to the big rock on the edge of their little camp site. "I been thinkin' a lot about you, Kid. We're not that different, you and me. I think you'd be a hard worker and a good fit in a lot of outfits around. Ranches and the like hire boys like you that can push cows and horses. What I'm sayin', Kid is I don't wanna leave you here to hit or miss. I want you to tag along with me till we find you a place to light."

Donnie's face lit up and he jumped up and said. "Aw Hunter do ya mean it?"

Hunter said. "I wouldn't have said it if I didn't mean it. Now saddle up, we got miles to make. We gotta stop in town and show this poster around."

They packed up their small camp and headed into town.

Past the livery there was a hardware store, which is to say a wood frame structure covered with canvas, a saloon with a red pair of bat-wing doors, and a general store. On the other side of the street were a saddle shop, a freighter's office, and the town hall. Hunter thought these folks a little ambitious, building a town hall for a cross-roads camp. It was their camp though; they could build whatever they damned well pleased. Hunter reigned up at the hardware store. He said, "Wait here, watch the horses."

Inside the store the owner was waitin' on and old man who was laboring over the decision of the one dollar or the two dollar shovel. The owner told him the shovels were the same, the handles were different. One was pine and weak, the other was hickory and a lot stronger. He could buy the cheaper one and come back in a week, and buy a hickory shovel handle for another dollar, his choice. While the old man had him busy, Hunter picked up one of the bushel baskets by the door and started collecting a few things - one tin coffee cup, one tin plate, another fork, a blanket, a small but serviceable hunting knife. Passing the glass gun case Hunter stopped in his tracks. Inside the case was a Colt Single Action Army. It had blued barrel and cylinder, case hardened frame, and someone had changed the grips out to a fine pair made of bone.

After the old man finally bought the one dollar shovel, the owner walked to Frank shakin' his head. "Help you, Sir?" Frank asked. "You take trades on these pistols, Mister?"

"Yup, although I'd rather take cash."

"I'd rather keep my cash if I can." Hunter allowed.

"Watcha got in mind?" The merchant asked.

Hunter pulled out the Schofield, "How would you trade on this for what's in the basket and that bone handled Colt?" Hunter thumbed the latch, broke the pistol over and dropped the five shells in his left hand. Then he handed it to the clerk. "Let me look at the colt if you will."

The man opened a squeaky wooden door on the back of the glass cabinet and handed Frank the pistol. He was in luck. It was a .44-40. The Cylinder locked up tight and the finish was unmarred save a little holster wear on the edge of the muzzle.

Frank spun the cylinder listening to the whirr. He then tried it in the cross draw holster. Nice fit. Frank would soak the holster in water tonight and tighten it up on the pistol. He laid it on the counter and said. "What'cha think?"

He could tell by the shop keepers face he fancied the Schofield, so did Frank it just wouldn't use the same ammo as the rest of his tools.

The shopkeeper looked in the basket adding the items in his head and said. "The Schofield and twenty."

Frank looked around the store and his eye lit on an old pair of saddlebags. "Throw in those saddlebags and you have a deal." The store owner agreed. Frank dug in his coat pocket and produced the last fourteen .45 Smith and Wesson cartridges he had. "Guess I don't need these anymore." he said. Then he dug in his hatband and fished out another twenty dollar gold piece. Three left. He had to catch Lowe in a hurry or he'd be broke. As the storekeeper stowed the purchases in the saddlebags Frank plucked five shells from his belt and loaded the colt. He holstered it and headed for the door.

Just as he reached the door he remembered why he came in here in the first place He fished the poster out of his shirt pocket. "While I'm here, have you seen this man?"

The merchant looked at it and said. "Sure have, he spent two night playing poker over to the saloon. He pulled out day before yesterday with three other fellas headed east."

"Much obliged." Hunter said and walked out.

That was fine. Even with the rain and the kid he still gained a day on ol' David Lowe. He didn't think anyone was comin' for him. Let him keep on thinkin'. He might even stop a couple of nights in Webber's Falls with his new friends. If he did, Frank would have him draped across his saddle on his way to the nearest U.S. Marshal's office to put in for the reward and look for a ranch that needed a good young hand.

Donnie was waiting with the horses just where Hunter had left him. He stopped short and opened the saddlebags pulled out the blanket and the knife. He tossed the bag to the boy and said. "Tie that on your horse." He rolled the blanket and opened his own saddlebag and produced a two foot piece of rawhide lacing. He cut in two with the new knife. It was good and sharp. "Tie the bedroll on with this and put this knife on your belt." Hunter told him. He watched him tie the laces in perfect knots. The kid had good hands.

"We caught a break. Lowe stayed here two days. He's only two days ahead of us now."

Donnie pulled the knife from the scabbard. He said. "Thanks for the knife Hunter. No one ever give me nothin' in my life till I met you."

Frank scowled and said. "Shut up kid. Remember my Pop." They rode in silence for three hours, Hunter thinkin' his thoughts and Donnie smiling and adoring the bounty hunter from twenty feet back on the trail. In a couple of days his adoration would become tinged with fear at what the man's hands were capable of.

That night the boy hunted while Hunter built the fire and started coffee. The coffee was done and Hunter was having some in his old cup. He had the new one on the rock by the fire for the kid. He heard the twelve gauge bark in the woods sounded like a half mile away. Directly Donnie walked into camp with two fat cottontails already skinned and dressed. He said. "They were dumb enough to crouch there together so I got em both with one shot."

Hunter set about fryin' them as the kid cleaned his gun. After they ate, Hunter had a sip of the bourbon while the boy rinsed out the skillet and the plate. Then he rolled out his new blanket, checked the shotgun to be sure it was loaded, leaned it against the tree by his bed. He said. "G'night Hunter."

Hunter said. "Get some sleep. And no sleepin' in tomorrow." The boy laid his head on his saddle, folded the top half of the blanket over him and was asleep in minutes. Frank had another sip and turned in himself.

The next morning Hunter woke about an hour before the dawn to the smell of coffee brewing. He smiled before he opened his eyes. This boy would be fine on a ranch. He had already saddled his horse. Hunter was amazed that the kid did all this without waking him. Usually a raccoon walking by the camp roused him out of a sleep; this kid must be quiet as a Comanche. They had their coffee then Hunter saddled his gelding while the kid put away the pot and cups. Then he smothered the fire with dirt.

"I'm Ready." he said to Hunter. They left without another word.

Chapter 6 – Trouble on the Trail

Hunter and the kid rode in silence. The only sounds were birds, hooves, and the creak of leather. Hunter was in the lead and Donnie in the rear. They were making good time. They were crossing the big valley that would someday become Lake Eufaula. All day Hunter had the feeling that someone was watching him, or them, as now was the case . He couldn't tell from where but he could feel it. He found out in the war that this feeling was seldom wrong. He turned to the kid and said. "Keep your eyes and ears open. Someone's watchin' us I can feel it." Then he just turned back and kept on ridin'.

They made camp that night in a little cedar grove by a stream that bubbled down toward the Canadian River. Frank shot a pair of squirrels and gave them to Donnie along with the skillet, the salt, and pepper. He said. "Your turn tonight boy", and walked down to the creek. When he got there he unbuckled his gun belt and slid the cross draw holster off the rig. He leaned over and dropped it in the water. He started pickin' up deadfall for the fire. He strapped on the belt with just the right hand holster with the old Colt in it. He took the wood up to the camp and headed back to the creek. He retrieved the holster from the water. Back at camp he slung as much excess water out of the holster as he could and set it down. After they ate the squirrels (which were delicious) and the coffee was brewing Hunter put the new Colt on his lap and produced the little canvas bag from his saddlebag. He oiled the whole exterior of the pistol including the grips and pushed it into the shrinking leather holster. It was soft and pliable as Frank took his thumbs and pressed the leather into all the contours of the gun. He pressed in at the bottom of the cylinder frame and the cylinder flutes until you could see the colt through the leather. He set it aside close to the fire to dry. Not too close though, he needed it close to him because that watched feelin' was still with him, maybe even stronger.

After the coffee Donnie asked Hunter if he still felt them.

"Yup, they're there alright. Once I thought I smelled them. At least one of them is a buffalo hunter. Go to sleep kid but sleep with one eye open. They probably won't come till morning. They're tired too." At that Hunter laid his head on his saddle and dosed, but heard everything. Around midnight the fire was nothin' but a pile of embers he stoked it back up and checked the cross draw holster. It was dry and tight on the Colt. He started pulling the pistol out and pushing it back into the holster. When the fit was right he slid the holster back onto his rig and wiped down the Colt and re-oiled it. He spent some time making sure he got all the oil off the bone grips.

They were up and makin' coffee the next morning when the three watchers walked up to the camp. Hunter smelled the buff hunter a hundred yards away and was on his guard. They cleared the brush cedars and into the clearing when he heard Donnie gasp. "Preston!"

"I oughta kill you, Boy" this old man yelled. His pards had guns on Frank when they walked up. One had a Remington .44 the other an old Sharps rifle, .50 caliber, Hunter judged by the cavern opening up at the rifles muzzle. Frank also saw that neither one of ol' Preston's partners came here for killin'. Neither of them had their pieces cocked and Preston hadn't even pulled his gun from the holster he was headed to give Donnie a beatin' ."I hired these two to track you're little ass and it took us long enough."

"Don't do it, Mister" Hunter barked. The old man whacked Donnie a good one across the nose and Hunters hands took over. He drew the old Colt in a blur, fanning the hammer. The tracker and Mr. I-CAN-SMELL-YOU-FROM-A-HUNDRED-YARDS went down. Three chest wounds in the buff hunter, two in the tracker. He dropped the old Colt where he stood and drew the new Colt from his left side and fanned the hammer twice and two red holes appeared in Preston's forehead. The whole exchange took three seconds. Hunter whispered. "I said don't do it."

Donnie looked around dazed. Not believing what he was seeing. Not believing what he saw. How could anybody be that fast and accurate, seven shots and seven hits in what seemed like a heartbeat.

Hunter picked up his cup and finished his coffee before it could get cold and poured another cup. "Leave 'em here, coyotes will take care of em for us. Won't change em much either, they'll still be shit." He reloaded the tools.

They packed up and were ready to leave when Donnie walked over and picked up the trackers .44 Remington. "Can I have it Hunter?"

"It's on you Donnie. Once you strap that thing on you're fair game to anyone with a pistol and an ugly temper. I wouldn't wear it till you can use it.

Donnie unbuckled the trackers belt and pulled it from under him. He holstered the Remington and rolled the belt up and stuffed it in his saddlebags.

Frank had him gather up the rest of the guns. "Can't leave em here for the Indians. Some will get up to mischief when they get in the bottle." Once the sharps was tied onto Hunter's saddle, they headed out. After a minute Frank didn't hear the kid behind him and he pulled the gelding around just in time to see the kid unbutton his fly and piss in the old trader's dead face. Frank smiled and thought to himself. "I guess that settles that," and rode on.

The boy rode behind Hunter a good ways for a while with his own thoughts occupying him. "How could Hunter be that fast with a gun? Is it something he learned? Is it something someone taught him?" There was no hesitation...Just a man dealing out the end of three men's lives like they were poker hands." Donnie was in awe of the man's hands, his reflexes, and his nerve. He was also a bit afraid. Any man that could do that must be evil at heart, but Donnie knew in his own heart that Hunter wasn't evil. He'd still keep an eye on him... and run if he needed to.

After a while he caught back up with Hunter and said. "I wanna thank you for killin' that son-of-a-whore Preston. The other two fellas I didn't know."

I didn't do it because of what he done to you in the past. That's done and over with. If his two pards hadn't had their guns on me I would have beaten the ol' bastard senseless. But when deadly force is brought to bear it can only be met with deadly force if you expect to survive in this country. I did it to stop the beatin' that was about to commence. I did warn him not to do it."

Donnie thought a long time about what Hunter had said. He was right about all that business with Preston bein' done and over with. He was also right about meetin' deadly force with deadly force. When it came down to it, Donnie couldn't find evil in anything Hunter had done...It was just the way he did it, like he was puttin' on his boots. No remorse, no regret, just a dirty job that had to be done before he could finish his coffee. And he DID warn him.

They ate polk salad that night for supper, boiled in that little skillet. Hunter said they needed some greens to clean the rabbit fat out of their guts. After they had their coffee while the fire guttered down. Hunter told Donnie some of his story. Some

of his story was his (and Marla's) only. Some of it he had
forgotten or blocked out. A lot of the war he lost. The rest he
would tell the kid, not all tonight though. They gotta sleep some
and it's a long story.

Chapter 7 – The Tellin's the Hard Part Pt.1

Frank started the story at the business with Pop and goin'
to Shreveport. The Irish Sergeant that got him into the army, Sgt.
Patrick O'Malley, also trained him at Ft. Monroe. "Laddys" he'd
say. "If a man pulls a gun on ya... Ya shoot him...If he pulls a
knife on ya... Ya shoot him... If he picks up a stone to hurl at ya...
Ya shoot him... If he raises his fists against ya... Ya kick his
friggin' arse. If a man brings deadly force to the fight me lads, by
God, meet it with the same. If a man wants a fist fight though,
oblige him. A fist fight is an honorable endeavor indeed. It
doesn't prove a friggin' thing me boys but who's face is harder.
I've lost lots of fist fights as ya can tell by me pretty and delicate
face." O'Malley's face was anything but pretty and delicate.
Before the war he'd been a warfman in New Orleans. He said
Nawlins like he was from the French Quarter but every other
word was pure Irish accent. He'd say "You Lassies wouldn't last
a minute on the docks in Nawlins. The rats would carry you off."
He was the toughest, hardest, killin'est man Hunter had ever
known. At camp there was always a smile on his lips but his eyes
always watched the tree line. He was never caught off guard. He
survived the war. Well most of him did.

A week before they surrendered the regiment, Hunter had
seen him in a hospital tent in Southwest Tennessee. His left leg
had been severed by a cannonball. He was still smiling. Frank
said. "Where the hell's yer leg O'Malley?"

The old Sergeant looked up and said. "Hunter me lad, I
knew you would make it home. You were the best listener I ever

trained. I always knew you understood what I was tryin' to say."

Frank said. "I only remembered to kill the ones that wanna kill me, and fight the ones that wanna fight me and, keep my eyes and ears open.

O'Malley thought a minute and said. "Frank, Son, that's all I had to say."

Just then a stout nurse with an enormous bosom walked past the cot and O'Malley reached out and slapped her formidable bottom.

She scowled at him and said "Sgt. O'Malley that kind of behavior will not be tolerated in this tent." She stomped off secretly smiling to herself.

O'Malley said. "She's goin' back to Nawlins with me. Might need a wee bit o' help with the leg, and, I believe she might need a wee bit o' help with those bosoms." They shared a laugh and Hunter had to be goin' up to Nashville.

Hunter said. "If I get down that way I'll look you up you old warhorse."

O'Malley said, "If ya do, the drinks are on you." They smiled and Frank walked away.

Hunter's story came back to Texarkana and the altercation between the three drunks at the Three Doors, and Marla. She saved him from hell that night. Killin' out of anger was a one-way road to damnation. Frank killed people who would be killed anyway. They had killed or stolen enough and those people would kill Frank if they could. Frank always gave them the first move. If they wanted to come peaceably they could, but they never did, not in this country.

Frank stayed on in Texarkana for a year. He found a few jobs. Feed store clerk; loading feed sacks on wagons. For a while he was a ranch hand out south of town. He even tended bar at the Three Door for a while. That couldn't last. He couldn't watch Marla go upstairs with all those cowboys and card players. When Frank wasn't working she was his, but when she was working, she was working. Frank only lasted a week.

Frank spent his free time and all his money at the Three Doors Saloon. They had sandwiches at the bar. If they hadn't he would have lived on beer alone. He was totally in love with Marla Anderson. She loved him too but, she was a realist and more than a little jaded for a girl of nineteen. She knew she had to work and the most money she could make was as a saloon girl.

Steve Sanders who owned the Three Doors was an ok guy. He didn't mind if she took the day off or left to be with Frank. He knew she'd come back. As long as he kept getting sixty cents out of every dollar she made, she could do what she wanted. Of course he charged her five dollars a week for her room plus her meals. Before Frank she usually cleared thirty bucks a week after her expenses were deducted. Steve got his sixty five and he was happy with that. Her customer count had been down lately since Frank had been around. Sanders still got his room rent and meal money. She still made him forty dollars a week. Not bad for doin' nothin but sendin' someone to change the sheets every other day.

Frank and Marla went on long rides, had picnics, made love by the little creek on Franks land. They were as in love as two people could be under the circumstances. Hell Frank still loved her now twenty years later. Thought of her every night when his head hit his saddle.

Marla had a baby the following July. A beautiful dark-haired girl. Marla named her Becca. Marla wrote her sister in St. Louis, Anna was her name. Anna came down and helped Marla out for a while. Frank could tell Marla was struggling with something and when he asked Marla told him. "Anna wants to take Becca back to St. Louis with her. Frank, what kind of life is here for her with a saloon girl Momma and a drifter Daddy." So together they decided Becca would go home with Anna. It was then that Frank went into town lookin' for a way to make more money.

Frank had been to the stage office and signed up to drive the stage. He had driven a six horse team in the army, weren't nothin' to it. He was walkin' by the town Marshal's office when he saw the poster. Hunter's first bounty was named Marcus Faulk. Frank couldn't remember what ol' Marcus had done but he remembered the reward was two hundred and fifty dollars, dead or alive. Hunter asked a couple of cowboys at the Three Doors if they knew him over a beer.

One of them said, "Sure I know him."

Hunter said, "You know where I can find him? I got something I gotta give him."

The cowhand allowed Marcus lived with his Momma Southeast of town on Wagner Creek. Frank lit out right then. He camped out that night on Wagner Creek. He cleaned the old Colts Dragoon by fire light. Tomorrow he would ride the road along the creek and ask around for Marcus Faulk. First light came and Hunter saddled up and rode north along the creek and met a man in his late twenties. Frank fingered the brim of his gray Confederate hat brim and said. "Mornin', you Marcus Faulk?"

"I am neighbor, who's askin'?"

Hunter said, "My name's Frank Hunter."

Faulk asked, "We got business Mr. Hunter?" Hunter said flatly. "I'm here to take you to the Marshal and collect the reward. I got a baby to care for and this is the only way I can get the money she needs, sorry Faulk."

Marcus says, "You ain't collected it yet, Boy." His right hand went to the rifle he had in a saddle scabbard. Franks hands took over. The big pistol cleared leather before Faulk really had a grip on the rifle. Frank thumb cocked the hammer and shot him once through the chest. Frank tied his hands to his feet under the belly of his horse, and took him to the Marshal's office.

The town Marshal in Texarkana was a big burly man in his forties. You could tell by his belly he liked his food and by the blood vessels in his face that he liked his whiskey. His name was Ledbetter. Marshal Ledbetter told Hunter to sell the horse, saddle, and his rifle, and bring the money back and split it with him. He would put in for the reward. Prob'ly take two weeks to get back.

Frank sold the horse and saddle at the livery for sixty dollars. He got fifteen for the Springfield at the hardware store. The split meant that Marshal Ledbetter got forty and Hunter got thirty five. Next time Hunter would get change before he went to make the split.

Hunter went to the Three Doors to see Marla. She was workin', but you could see the gloom in her heart. He gave her twenty of the thirty five dollars he had and told her there would be more. "I am going to bring you a hundred and twenty five in a couple a weeks." She knew Frank, he wouldn't rob anyone or steal. He was a lot of things but a thief wasn't one of them. She didn't ask where he got it or what it was for. She would mail it to St. Louis for Becca's care and upbringin'.

And so it started. Ten days later the Marshal gave him the reward money. Seems like they'd have given him a marker or a check but, it seemed like bounty rewards were a cash only business. Hunter plucked another poster off the wall at the Marshal's office and went to settle up with Marla. He told her to keep what she needed and send the rest to St. Louis. She did then, and with every bounty Hunter collected for the last 19 years. She could have quit at the Three Doors but it was all she knew.

The next day Hunter lit out after the name on the poster. He told Marla she could have the house, but she wouldn't move out there alone. Frank knew she would stay at the Three Doors. It was her home. He told her he'd be back as soon as he could but didn't know when that would be.

"That's enough for one night." Hunter told Donnie who had been listening to every word of the story like it was the Gospel straight from the mouth of John.

He asked. "Half of every bounty for nineteen years? How much have you sent her Hunter?"

Hunter said. "None of your business.......twelve thousand and fifty dollars... go to sleep".

Chapter 8 – Webber's Falls

The sun caught them both sleeping the next morning. After dinner Frank must have talked for four or five hours. He was sure it was the most he had talked at any one sitting in his life. Felt good to have it off his chest.

Frank judged that if they stayed movin' they'd reach Webber's Falls tonight. Hunter had been there before. It was a settlement and trading post on the East edge of the Territories. It was set up at a narrow spot on the Arkansas River. There was a ferry there to cross the river. Frank would pay the fare after he had Lowe bundled and rigged for travel.

They called it Webber's Falls because some old Cherokee chief named Webber opened the tradin' post there back in the sixties. The Arkansas rolled over a rock ledge there and dropped about a foot. Not really much of a fall at all. The Confederate Army kept a post there for a while during the War. Hunter had never come this far west in his duties. His duties kept him more north and east.

They could see the lights of Webber's Falls when they camped that night. Hunter didn't want to go in while it was dark. He liked to be able to see what he was up against if he could. He sat by the fire and cleaned his tools. He even sharpened his knife. He gave Donnie' s knife a rub on the rock too. It really didn't need it, he just wanted to keep busy till bedtime. He laid down about an hour after dark. He had no trouble sleeping. He was ready. He thought.

Next morning they went into town. They rode slow down the one muddy street. Frank saw the boarding house was close to the saloon. "Handy for the drunks." He thought. Across the street there was a cafe. Hunter could use another cup of coffee and he bet the boy had never had breakfast at a cafe. They reigned up and Hunter said, "Let's grab some breakfast." They tied their horses at the rail and went in.

Hunter sat at a table near the front of the cafe lookin' out the window. He fished the poster out of his pocket. The waitress came. She was a feisty little red head with freckles all over her face and arms. Frank thought prob'ly everything else too. O'Malley had always said, "Boys, happiness is a girl with freckles on her tits"

"Coffee gents?" She asked. Frank and Donnie both nodded. She came back with the coffee and asked. Whatcha eatin'?"

Hunter said. "We both want bacon with eggs over easy and biscuits".

"Comin' right up". She said on her way to the kitchen. Apparently she was waitress and cook. They could hear her back there bangin' the pans.

Hunter sat there sippin' his coffee and watchin' the street. Occasionally he would unfold the poster and look Lowe's features over. It was around nine in the morning and loyal patrons were already arriving at the saloon across the way. It was called the Lucky 7 Saloon and Gambling Hall. It was a shoddy built structure. Two stories and you could tell the winter wind blew right through it. Winters in the Territories were short but they were damned cold sometimes. The outside of the saloon was whitewashed and the bat-wing doors were stained but worn at the tops where so many dirty hands had pushed them open.

Their breakfast came and the redhead refilled their coffee. Frank ate and watched. Donnie, who hadn't ever eaten breakfast in a cafe, was in heaven. He was stuffing the bacon in and sopping up the runny egg yolk with a biscuit. He had a little yolk on his chin.

The girl filled their coffee again and said. "Getcha anything else gents?"

"Nah, I think we're done." Hunter said without looking around. Lowe was walking into the Lucky 7. "What's the Damage."

The redhead said six bits apiece. Frank went onto his pocket for the folding money and gave the girl two dollars and said. "Keep the change Red."

Must've been the first fifty cent tip she'd ever gotten. She looked at Frank and said. "Thanks so much Mister." Hunter sat in the chair a moment while he pulled the old Colt and put a bullet in the sixth chamber then did it with the new Colt.

Outside Hunter said "Wait here, Boy." and walked across the street without looking back. He walked into the dim light of the Lucky 7 and went to work. He crossed to the bar and ordered a beer he didn't intend to drink and laid a dollar on the bar like he intended to drink nine more. Lowe was sitting at a table with three of his friends, playin' cards and talkin' about the hair of the dog that bit 'em. Must have been a big night last night. After Hunter's eyes fit the light he looked the place over. Lowe's table was against the back wall, in the corner by the window. Frank would have his back to the bartender and the front door when he took Lowe. Hunter didn't like it, but as of now they didn't know he was after Lowe at all. Lowe wouldn't stay and play poker if he knew someone from Texas was after him.

After a few minutes Hunter moved across the room so he was directly in front of Lowe and said, "You David Lowe?"

"Depends on who's asking." He replied.

"My name's Frank Hunter and I'm takin' you to the Federal Marshal in Ft. Smith and collect the reward those Texans put on you for killin' their constable."

Donnie sat on the step at the cafe. The redheaded girl brought him out a glass of cool buttermilk. He'd never had buttermilk. It was half gone and he still didn't know if he liked it. It had a tang to it he wasn't sure of. He was sippin' it when a tall, stocky man came out of the boarding house and headed for the Lucky 7. Donnie saw him peer through the door and pull his pistol before he went through the doors quiet as a mouse.

Frank stood there waiting to see what Lowe and his friends were gonna do. He couldn't tell if they were good enough friends to fight for him. They looked like they would have turned him in for the reward if they'd known there was one. Frank had done this enough to know you really couldn't tell till the guns were pulled. It was right about then that he heard the three distinct clicks of a Colt revolver being cocked directly behind him. He heard a big deep voice say.

"Keep them hands away from them pistols Bounty Hunter. I don't know him and I don't know you, but, I ain't gonna stand for no bounty hunters in Webber's Falls".

When it happened the hackles stood up on Hunter's neck he knew he was beat when a boom that sounded like one of the cannons from the War went off right behind him. Lowe and his buddies dove under the table. Hunter stood still to see if he was gonna fall down, when he didn't, he turned to find Donnie reloading his shotgun and the big voiced guy nearly cut in half at the waist. Donnie had stuck the barrels between the bat wings and pulled both triggers. Hunter could hear the other four scrambling he turned just as they were pulling iron. His hands took over.

As they got up the man on the far right was pulling. Hunter pulled the old Colt and fanned the hammer twice, one in the head and one in the chest. Lowe was hurling himself at the window, but, the far left buddy was clearing leather. It seemed as though when hunter was in a gun fight time slowed down so Hunter could see with great clarity what needed to be done next. He fanned the hammer two more times, and the guy on the left's nose imploded on his face, just as Lowe crashed through the glass and into the alley behind the Lucky 7. The other buddy wasn't as good a friend as the first two because his hands went straight up. Frank walked out the door and around the back as buddy number three ran from the saloon and back to the boarding house. Hunter looked long and hard both ways down the alley... no sign of him. He went back inside.

Donnie stood there with his shotgun looking a little remorseful. He also looked alive. Surviving a gunfight always gave a man the feeling that he was really alive. Hunter knew it was because you were an instant away from feeling dead. Hunter bent and picked the big man's head up by the hair. He looked at Donnie and said, "There's paper on this bastard." He looked at the barkeep and said, "Sell their guns and boots and pay for their burial, or sell their guns and boots and drag them off into the woods I don't give a shit. But the money for their guns and boots is all you're getting." Frank took the money from the poker table and put it in his coat pocket. He told Donnie to get the horses.

After Donnie had gone Hunter asked the bartender if he knew the big guy.

He allowed that it was Big Jim Barrington. He was wanted in Missouri, and Arkansas. He holed up here in Webber's Falls and killed every bounty hunter that came lookin' for him. He'd killed three so far.

Hunter said. "Well I betcha he don't kill another." At that Hunter bent and looked at Big Jim's pistol. Damn .45 Colt. He tossed it to the bartender. "You can sell this one too. He grabbed big Jim's foot and dragged him out of the Lucky 7 and into the muddy street.

Donnie brought the horses back across the way and Hunter looped his rope around Big Jim's feet and mounted up. He dallied the rope around the saddle horn and headed for the livery. When they got there Hunter asked the livery man if he knew ol' Big Jim Barrington.

He said, "Sure everybody knows Big Jim."

Hunter said, *"Knew* Big Jim… Did he keep a horse here?"

Liveryman said, "He sure did. Back Stall on the left."

Hunter said, "Saddle him up he's gotta carry him a little bit further. What's his bill gonna cost me?"

The hostler said, "Two dollars. Big Jim paid up Friday."

Hunter paid the man with two silver dollars he took from the poker table. While he saddled Big Jim's horse Hunter went out to talk to Donnie.

"What you did back there was save my life. I don't often need it but I am damned sure glad you were there when I did, Donnie. Thank you."

Donnie looked up a little teary eyed and said. "I seen him come out of that boarding house and peek in the saloon door. He pulled out his pistol, and I knew if I yelled out he would 'a shot you . It was all I could think to do."

"You did just fine Donnie. Now I got an errand for you to run while I finish up here." Hunter went into his pocket and pulled out the poker table money. He started counting it, came to one-hundred-forty-six dollars all paper currency except for the six silver dollars. Hunter handed Donnie three silver dollars. Donnie's eyes lit up. Then hunter handed him a fifty and a twenty dollar bill. "Seventy-three dollars. That's your half. If we are gonna be partners you need to get your share. Go down to the hardware and buy two boxes of .44-40 bullets. I think it will take a couple of boxes to get you shootin' that Remington well enough to wear, also we need a box of six shot twelve gauge shells if you are gonna keep shootin' 'em up two at a time. Remember kid, at six feet a shotgun is the best weapon you can have. At sixty it'll just make 'em mad."

"Hunter?" Donny asked. "Can I buy somethin' for me at the hardware?"

Hunter replied, "It's your money I don't give a shit what you do with it." Donnie mounted up and headed back up the street.

Hunter turned his attention back to the liveryman. "Did this fella have a horse here." Hunter asked while showing him the wanted poster.

The hostler said "He did for a fact. Just came and got him after the shootin we heard. I never seen anyone saddle a horse that fast. He lit out south."

Hunter asked which stall his horse was in. The liveryman showed him. Hunter went down on one knee. He looked at the horse tracks in the dirt in the livery floor. O'Malley had taught him that you can't track a man on horseback. You track a horse. Ya gotta find somethin' different in his hoof print. Hunter found what he was looking for in a minute. The left rear hoof had five

nails in it, three on the left and two on the right all the rest had
six nails. If Lowe didn't have his horse shod Hunter could track
him. Probably wouldn't be for a week or ten days. They had to
go to Ft. Smith and put in for the reward on Big Jim.

Donnie went into the hardware store and told the clerk
what he was after. The clerk was a boy about Donnie's age. He
gathered it up. Donnie scanned the stock in the store lookin for
something he wanted. He'd never had money of his own to buy
something he wanted. Now that he had some he couldn't think
of anything he needed. He paid for the ammo and left. He
stopped at the general store next. He bought two cans of new
potatoes, two cans of carrots, two cans of sweet cling peaches
and an onion. He would surprise Hunter with a stew tonight
with peaches for dessert. He stowed them in his saddlebags and
went back to the livery just as Frank was tying Big Jim's hands
under his saddle. He had a length of rope around what was left
of his middle tied to the saddle horn.

Frank said "When we get to Ft. Smith you should trade Ol'
Jim there saddles. He won't be needin' his anymore anyway and
it's a damned nice saddle."

Hunter told Donnie they'd take Big Jim into Ft. Smith put
in for the reward and sleep in beds for a few days. In Ft. Smith
the money could be wired in, they didn't have to wait for the
mails to run. The telegraph was a wonderful thing unless you
were an outlaw. You can't outrun the telegraph.

They mounted up and headed for the ferry crossing. The
man that operated the ferry said. "Two bits for a horse and rider,
even if the rider ain't breathin'." Hunter gave the man fifty cents.

The ferryman looked at Donnie. When it dawned on
Donnie he was waitin' on his fare he said "Sorry sir. I was
thinkin' of somethin' else." He dug in his pocket and came out
with a quarter. He was proud and happy to pay his way. He had
no idea he was ten days away from more money than he had
even seen in Ol' Preston's strong box.

Chapter 9 – Ft. Smith

They crossed the Arkansas River and continued east, the boy who had killed his first man and the man who had killed one hundred and twenty three. As they rode Frank thought about the way the kid had handled it. He was kind of taken aback but not too disturbed about the fact that he had ended a man's life this morning and now the body of that man was draped over the horse the kid was leading along the steep hilly trail from Webber's Falls to Ft. Smith, Arkansas. The night would tell. If he was disturbed, his dreams would betray him in the night.

Around noon they stopped at a stream to water the horses and themselves, didn't even offer Big Jim a swallow. He was startin' to smell and Donnie was havin' a hard time stayin' upwind in these hills. As they sat there on a big rock Donnie asked Hunter, "Hunter, shouldn't I feel worse about shootin' that outlaw in the back?"

Hunter thought about it a minute and said, "Well first of all if you hadn't I'm sure he would have killed me. Then if you tried to help he would have killed you. I believe he was gonna shoot me in the back, besides his back was toward you. Were you gonna ask him to turn around?"

The boy said, "I don't really feel bad about it at all Hunter. I think he had it coming."

Hunter nodded. "I know he had it coming, his kind always do. Ya know they don't put rewards on men's heads because they might have done something. He had it coming, and you gave him what he asked for."

They camped early that evening and Frank said, "We better hunt early because if you start practicing that pistol there won't be a rabbit within a mile of here." So they hunted. Both had a shotgun Hunter with his pistols. They bagged two rabbits and a squirrel. Back at camp Donnie produced the canned potatoes and carrots. He kept the peaches hid for a surprise. He

chopped the onion with the knife Hunter had given him. He
started cooking them with the rabbit and squirrel meat he had
cut from the bones. When they were starting to brown he added
a can of potatoes and a can of carrots. This filled the little fry pan.
He salted and peppered and simmered them for a while.

While the stew simmered Hunter told him. "Bring me that
Remington." Donnie went and got it out of the saddlebag and
handed it to Hunter. Hunter opened the loading gate. All six
chambers were loaded. Apparently the tracker had readied
himself for a fight just like Hunter had. He unloaded the pistol
and told the boy to sit down. He handed the unloaded revolver
to Donnie and told him to check it and see if it was loaded. He
did and verified it was clear. Hunter said to him, "That damned
thing is not a toy for a sixteen year old cowhand on a ranch to
shoot snakes and lame horses. It isn't some passage to manhood.
It is simply a tool, used to do the job of ending a man's life. If a
man is far enough away and he can't hit you with a pistol you
can hide or run...no killin's needed. If you can get out of the way,
do it. If you are close and have no cover and a man uses deadly
force toward you, jerk this pistol and kill him. Don't try to wing
him or leg-shoot him. If he's worth shootin' he's worth killin'. I
want you to listen to me now. I've been watchin' you and you
have good hands. They can learn this. First cock that pistol. Next
find a rock or pebble on the ground and dry fire at it."

"How many times?" Donnie asked.

"Oh about two thousand. While you do it, you watch the
front sight of that pistol. Try to keep the sight lined up all the
way through the shot after the hammer falls. When your hand
can do that every time, and you don't have to force it to do it,
we'll load that thing back up and you can shoot at something."

Donny started dry firing the Remington New Model at a
small red pebble at the edge of their camp.
Cock...click...cock...click. He did this while Hunter cleaned his
revolvers, Big Jim ripened, and the stew simmered. After a while
Donnie stirred and tasted. He said. "It's stew, let's eat it". It was

very good to have something besides fried rabbit or squirrel. They ate every bite. While the coffee brewed Donnie went to his saddlebags again and came back with the peaches. He offered a can to Hunter.

The man looked at Donnie and said, "Well ain't we all set with stew and dessert too." He took the can and opened it with his knife. He licked the stew off his fork and dug in. Frank couldn't remember the last time he'd had canned peaches. Had to be back before he left Texarkana. Marla liked 'em. He'd had plenty of money. He'd just never thought of buyin' any. He'd have to start rememberin'. These were damned good. When he'd finished eating them he turned the can up and drank the syrup... "Damned good, thanks for the peaches Donnie." He said.

Donnie smiled and said "You're welcome Hunter."

After the coffee Donnie cleaned up the supper mess. Hunter started cleaning his tools. He'd only fired one of them but he cleaned all three pistols anyway. Donnie continued to dry fire the Remington for a while longer. Hunter told him. "If you can stand the smell go pull the gun belt off Ol' Big Jim back there. It's in better shape than the one you have". Donnie went out in the dark. The horses were tied out in a little grass patch about twenty yards downwind of the camp. He came back with it. Hunter told him to put it around his waist. Hunter eyeballed the buckle and the length of the belt. He grabbed a twig from the fire and marked a couple of marks on the belt and took it off Donnie. He said. "Go back to yer practicin'."

Hunter looked at his marks and went to work with his knife. First trimming the excess off, but not too much he believed Donnie would fill out a bit. He'd already started some, even on one meal a day. After he'd trimmed the length he got a piece of the deadfall wood they'd gathered and used it for a backing while he punched holes. After he made sure the buckle worked in all the holes, he had Donnie try it on. It fit him perfect. The Remington had the same basic outline as the Colt that used to reside in the holster, unlike the Schofield. Hunter didn't think this one needed the water treatment. Even though he knew it would get it the first time it rained. Aside from the different ejector setup on the Remington it was the same size and shape as the Colt.

Hunter took the belt back and took all the .45 shells out and tossed them into the trees. There were twenty four loops on the belt and twenty four shells in them. Hunter put eighteen .44-40s back in the belt out of his saddlebag and gave it to Donnie who immediately put it on. He holstered the empty revolver. He drew and dry fired at the pebble. Hunter watched, more than a little taken aback by the speed of the boy's hands. He said, "Everybody's worried about how fast they can draw. It doesn't matter if you don't hit what you're shootin' at. Draw it fast and throw it if you can't hit with it. You understand me, Boy?"

"Yes I do." Donnie answered. He sat back down and dry fired for a little while longer then they both turned in. They would reach Ft. Smith tomorrow. Donnie was excited it would be the biggest town he'd ever been in.

The next day passed without much happening except Big Jim smellin' worse by the hour. They came to the ferry landing about an hour before sunset. Ft. Smith is built in a bend of the Arkansas River. The river protects three sides of the town. You don't have to cross the river if you come in from the South. They paid their fare for three horses and riders and went across.

Hunter went straight to the Marshal's office. He'd been here before a few times. The Marshal was a big fair man name Mike Buck. Marshal Buck had been in Ft. Smith a long time. Hunter had been in here sixteen or seventeen years ago and Buck had been here then. He was a deputy back then but was the Federal Marshal now.

Hunter told the boy to watch the horses; someone's liable to lead our payday off for the horse. Donnie watched standing by his horse with a hand on the butt of his shotgun. They wouldn't get it easy he thought.

Hunter stepped into the Marshal's office. In it were four

small desks and one big one. The small ones were for the deputies to do their reports and paperwork. The big one was for the Marshall. He was a big man, six-four, two hundred and fifty pounds. He sat at the desk drinkin' coffee. He looked up and said. "I'll be damned, Frank Hunter. Who's dead out there on their horse?"

Frank said, "Just because I wanted to say hello to an old friend someone's gotta be dead on their horse?...... Big Jim Barrington."

Marshall Buck said. "No shit? He's killed every bounty hunter that went into Webber's Falls for the last two years. He even killed one of my deputies I sent in there. How'd you get him.

"I baited him with my back and a sixteen year old boy shot him with a shotgun".

Buck looked at Hunter's face to see if he was being shitted or not. Satisfied hunter was on the level he said, "Let's go look at him shall we?" Hunter went out followed by the Marshall. "Whew"! Buck gasped. "You could'a killed him in February couldn't you?"

"Nah" Hunter said. "Would have been too easy."

Buck picked up his head by the hair and said. "Yup... That's Big Jim alright. I'll wire off for the reward tomorrow mornin'. It'll take a day or two to get back ya know."

"Yeah I know. We need a couple days rest anyway."

Marshall Buck saw Donnie standin' on the other side of the horses and said. "Who is that unsavory lookin' individual?" Frank told Donnie to come over and introduced him to the Marshall. He told the Marshal that Donnie didn't know his last name. Buck said he'll have to have one in the reward application. Frank said. "Well then just tell them it's Hunter too."

"Donnie Hunter the bounty hunter." Buck said, "Frank you're a poet and didn't know it."

Buck went to the door of the office and yelled inside at two deputies coming from back in the cells. "Roll him up in a blanket and get him down to the undertaker's before he falls off that horse".

They set about it and as soon as he was off Frank said. "Buck we're gonna find a room and sleep in a bed. Don't look for us too early."

They went to the livery hoping he wasn't closed up for the night. He wasn't. Hunter said. "First we need to board these two horses with you. They've been on the trail with nothin' but grass for a spell so give em some grain but not too much. Give em a good curry and turn em out in the corral. We'll be here three days or so. If we're here longer we'll come settle up then."

The liveryman said, "Sounds good Gents, what else can I do ya for?"

Hunter looked over at Donnie and asked. "Do you want that saddle? It's a lot newer than yours?"

Donnie looked it over and some goo had leaked out of Big Jim on it and he said, "Nah, I guess I'll just keep mine."

"I'd like to sell this horse and rig. What'll you give me for him?" Jim's horse was a big four or five year old quarter horse gelding.

"Good lookin' animal." The hostler allowed, "I can buy him from you but I gotta be able to make a buck on him too."

"I realize that mister I just don't have time to look for a buyer."

"Sixty five for the horse, saddle, and tack."

Hunter frowned a little so the liveryman would think he was getting' the best of him and said. "I guess you got me over a barrel mister... sold." The old man got a little metal box from under the shelf in the corner and counted out sixty five dollars. Hunter said. "How much for the three days board on our other two horses?"

The hostler replied, "Five dollars." Hunter handed back the five dollar bill. Donnie and him led their horses into the barn and tied them to a post. Hunter repeated, "Curry them and not too much grain."

"Yes sir." The liveryman replied.

As they walked back up the street Hunter handed Donnie thirty dollars. "Here's your half partner." Donnie took it thinking. He still had over sixty of the seventy three he'd gotten in Webber's Falls. This was the most money he'd ever seen. He had over ninety dollars. How the hell would he ever spend ninety dollars... Still didn't have a clue.

They went into a boarding house about a block from that Marshal's office. There were vacancies and Hunter told the clerk he needed two rooms.

The clerk said very quickly, as if he'd rattled of this sentence a thousand times, "A dollar a night, supper's at seven sharp, breakfast at seven sharp, for lunch you're on your own."

Hunter said. "Sounds fair. We'll be here two nights." He paid the man. Donnie didn't need reminding he had his two dollars already out. They got their keys and upstairs they went. Hunter said. "Stow your saddlebags and let's get cleaned up."

"I didn't see no creek around here," Donnie said.

Hunter said, "Just stow the bags." They walked a spell and found what hunter was lookin for. The sign said BATH HOUSE. Hunter led the way in.

There were oriental girls hauling hot water from the stove to the tubs. There were six bath tubs lined down the center of a long room. Three of them were occupied by guys that definitely needed a bath. Along the back wall were mirrors and a barber chair. Hunter found the owner, a small oriental woman.

She said, "Bath fifty cent, soap ten cent, shave one dolla.

Hunter said, "I want a bath with soap and a shave."

The owner snapped, "One dolla sixty cent." Hunter gave her two bucks. "Keep the change." He walked to an empty tub and started hangin' his clothes on a peg there.

Donnie said, "I need a bath with soap but I don't need no shave."

She said, "Sixty cent pretty boy."

Donnie was a little uncomfortable undressing in front of all the oriental women in the bath house. They didn't seem to know the men were there. They kept their eyes down and stayed busy. One of them brought Frank and Donnie each a new cake of lye soap each and started filling the tubs with hot water. Another came to help with the water hauling and in a few minutes they were up to their necks in steaming hot water. It felt great. Hunter bathed every time he came to town. This was another first for Donnie, bathing in a real bath tub. He bathed in a washtub in the cold months, standing up with a rag and in a creek if it was warm, but never more than once every other week.

Hunter looked across at him and said. "It's nice to wash your ass from time to time, makes it easier to spend time with yourself. In the morning we'll buy a new suit of clothes and maybe a spare pair of drawers to carry in the saddlebag. Never can tell when you're gonna need clean drawers."

After Hunter's bath he got up and went to the barber chair with just a towel around his waist. One of the girls came back and lathered up his face and gave him a shave. He was clean except for the mustache he kept. It was full and long on the sides all the way down on his neck. Frank thought it made him look mean.... He wasn't wrong.

After the shave they went to a restaurant and had supper with plates, and knives, and water in a glass. Hunter had roast beef, mashed potatoes and gravy, and apple pie. Donnie had a chicken fried steak, spuds and pie as well. Best meal he had ever eaten. After they ate they went to the boarding house. They went to their rooms, undressed and slept in a bed with sheets and a handmade quilt on top. Another first for the kid, he was liking this way of life more and more all the time.

Around eight the next morning Donnie came downstairs to find Hunter in the parlor drinking coffee.

He said. "You missed breakfast.... Seven sharp remember?"

Donnie said. "I needed the sleep more. Besides I'm still full from that supper last night".

They left the boarding house and looked for a clothing

store. They each bought two pairs of long handles, a cotton shirt and jeans and two pairs of socks. They paid up and went back to the boarding house and changed. They stowed the extra long handles and socks and headed to the Marshal's office.

They walked into the office and there sat Marshal Buck in his big chair behind his big desk drinking coffee. Hunter said, "Oughta known a gov'ment employee would just be sittin' around drinkin' coffee."

Buck shot back, "You clean up pretty good Frank. You lookin' to marry a widow here in Ft. Smith?"

Frank said. "Not likely."

Buck continued, "I already wired off for the money on Big Jim. I need you two to sign the forms to make it all legal and honest."

"What was on his head anyway Mike? I wasn't after him when he just fell in our laps, or on the floor of the Lucky 7 as the case may be."

Buck looked at Hunter and the kid for a moment and asked, "You don't know the bounty?"

"Sure don't, just recognized the name from somewhere." Hunter replied.

Buck looked them up and down again and said, "Well I told you he'd killed three bounty hunters and a deputy U.S. Marshall in the last two years didn't I?" Hunter allowed it was so. Buck said, "The bounty on Big Jim Barrington is eighteen hundred dollars." Frank never flinched. He just said. "Where do I sign?"

He signed his sheet and Donnie signed his after practicing it on a scrap a couple of times.

"Donnie Hunter" sounded strange to him. Donnie knew how to read and write because ol' Preston had wanted him to keep inventory on the stock while he would drink with the Indians wherever they were camped.

After they were done with the Marshall they went to find a place to kill time. They found a small saloon up the street. No girls, no Faro table. Pick up poker was being played on two of the six tables in the room. Hunter ordered a beer and so did the kid. They sipped in silence for a while then the kid broke the silence with one question that Hunter knew was coming.

"Did he say eighteen HUNDRED DOLLARS?"

Hunter said flatly, "Yup, he sure did".

The boy said. "Half of that's nine hundred dollars. I could live for years on that. Do you carry that around when you get that much money?"

Hunter replied. "I don't know. That's the biggest bounty I ever collected. I can tell you what I do. Like I said, I give half of all my bounties to Marla for Becca's upbringin', and to take care of Marla when she needs it. I have an account in the bank at Texarkana I'll wire the money down to those two accounts from the bank here in Ft. Smith except for three hundred and thirty dollars."

"Why three hundred and thirty dollars?" The boy asked.

Hunter said, "My hatband will hold fourteen twenty dollar gold pieces. I will get fifty dollars in small bills to keep in my pocket. The rest I split between Marla's and my account in the Bank of Texarkana".

The boy asked if he could open an account in Texarkana from here.

Hunter replied, "Let's go to the telegraph office and see." On the way they stopped and Donnie bought a proper Stetson hat. He threw away the old abused farmers hat he had. The hat had a back to front slope on the crown with the brim pulled low on the front, with room in the band for fourteen twenty dollar gold pieces.

They got to the telegraph office. Hunter sent a wire to the president of the Bank of Texarkana. He asked if it were possible to open an account over the wire, and if so what did he need to do. After about a half hour wait the message came back that they certainly could open an account over the telegraph. They needed to have the money to open the account given to the bank in Ft.

Smith and have his account information sent along with the money. He also needed somebody in Texarkana to be the other signature on the account. They had to have someone there to actually see to the business of the account. Hunter told him that he could trust Marla to take care of it if he decided to do this. They could wire her and ask her, if he wanted. Donnie said he did. Hunter sat down and took a sheet from the message tablet and began to write.

To: Marla Anderson
Where: Three Doors Saloon – Texarkana, Texas
From: Frank Hunter
Message: Marla I hope this telegram finds you alright – stop – I have kinda gained a partner up in the Territories -stop – He wants to open an account in the Bank of Texarkana like I have -stop- Will you do his business there for him like you do for me -stop- His name is Donnie Hunter -stop- It's a long story I'll tell you when I get home next -stop – we'll wait for your answer - stop- All my love Frank -stop

He handed it to the telegraph operator.
The clerk added the words and said. "It'll be six bits sir."
Hunter handed the guy a dollar. He sent the message and asked Hunter and Donnie to wait outside. He had to lock up for a few minutes he had two telegrams he had to deliver to the bank and the Marshal. He'd be back in five minutes. Hunter and Donnie waited on a bench outside the telegraph office. He was back in four but Marla's message was twenty minutes getting back.
It simply said: OK -stop- Love you too –stop. It must have been busy at the Three Doors.
Hunter and Donnie walked up the street to the Marshal's office and went inside. Buck looked at the kids new hat and said,

"That oughta hold fourteen twenty dollar gold pieces."

Donnie looked at Hunter. Hunter said. "He won't tell no one you got em."

Buck said, "Reward's already in. Bank should already have it split up in two piles for ya."

Frank said, "Much obliged Mike. We're pulling out at first light in the morning. I know you sleep late. If your gonna be here a while, we'll do our business, get some dinner and I'll come back and jaw with you a little while."

Marshal Buck said, "You bring the whiskey Frank."

Hunter replied, "Agreed. It's a date. Sad thing is you're the prettiest date I've had in six months."

Buck smiled and said, "Bet it's been longer than that."

They went down to the bank, signed the papers, and got their money. The bank manager asked where they had come by so much cash.

Hunter said, "We killed Big Jim Barrington for the reward." The manager asked which one of them got him. Hunter threw a thumb at the boy.

The bank manager reached into the safe and brought out a brand new hundred dollar bill and said. "This is for you. Jim Barrington robbed this very Bank and killed a teller who had been working here ten years. I am glad he's dead and I'll add a little to your share."

Donnie looked at it for a second and then asked the manager if he could break it. He said, "We're partners, everything splits down the middle."

Hunter gained a little respect for the kid there in the banker's office. Honor wasn't something you teach. You have it or you don't.

The bank transfers went smoothly. The bank manager said he would personally wire the transfer and new account information to Texarkana today. They took their Three hundred and thirty dollars each and left the bank. They ate in the same restaurant that they ate in the night before. After they'd finished

Hunter said, " I'm going back up to the Marshal's and talk old times. You're welcome if you want."

Donnie said, "I think I'll walk around a while. I'll see you back at the boarding house." They went their separate ways.

Hunter stopped in the small saloon he'd had a beer in the night before. He told the barkeep he wanted a bottle of his best bourbon.

He produced a bottle he said was smooth Kentucky sippin' whiskey.

He said, "Barkeep, if it ain't smooth I'll be back in a few minutes."

The bartender stopped him and traded him for a bottle from under the bar. He said, "Two dollars."

Hunter paid the man. If it was smooth it was worth two dollars. As it turned out it was very smooth.

Donnie walked along the streets of Ft. Smith. Looking through the store fronts, wishing he could think of something he needed. Then he realized he had new clothes and a new hat. He needed a new coat and boots. He started looking.

Hunter walked into the office holding a bottle. Buck said, "Did you threaten him?"

Hunter asked, "Why'd you ask me that?"

Buck said, "He won't sell a bottle of Buffalo Trace to me or anyone else. He saves it for himself." The two old friends talked about old times, talked about the Territories, talked about women. Buck knew about Marla and that neither of them was exclusive. He also knew that she was the only woman Hunter would ever love. He envied him that. Frank drank exactly three shots of the bourbon. It was smooth as advertised. Buck drank half the bottle.

Donnie found the boot shop. He went in and the shopkeeper fit him with a new pair of boots that were black bull hide. He told Donnie these would last him forever if he took care of them, have them resoled before the sides of the soles tattered. They set him back twenty dollars. Donnie wore them out of the store and went back to where he bought the jeans. He bought a lined denim coat, ten more dollars. He went back to the boarding house. He settled into his bed for the last time, it would be a couple of weeks before he would sleep indoors again. He savored it and played with the thirteen gold coins he had left. When he heard Hunter come in, Donnie dozed off.

When he woke he could hear Hunter packing his saddlebag in the next room. He poured water in the basin and splashed his face, dried off and started to get dressed. When he was packed he went downstairs. It was obviously seven sharp because breakfast was being served. It was big biscuits and sausage gravy, more sausage than gravy. It was a good meal to set out on.

After breakfast they walked down to the livery. Hunter said "Nice boots. Wondered when you'd think of em." The coat looks like a good one, too. Good shopping trip."

At the livery the hostler brought their horses in from the corral and tied them in stalls. They got their saddles from the rail and started saddling up.

When they were ready the old liveryman came around. Hunter asked, "We square?"

"Sure are," He answered. You boys be careful out on the trail. Anything can happen. Usually does."

They headed out of Ft. Smith to the south through the hills. In Hunter's mind he would pick up Lowe's trail at Talehina in the Winding Stair Mountains.

Chapter 10 – Back on the Trail

Once they cleared the edge of town and the small farms around the edge of Ft. Smith, Hunter started to feel a little more himself. Donnie on the other hand was just pissed off at himself because he hadn't thought to get some spurs. "All that time thinkin' about what he wanted and he never thought of spurs...Damn It!" South by Southeast was the general direction of their travel. Hunter had gone this way before several times. This was the route back home from Ft. Smith. About half way they would cut west and see if they could find Lowe's trail.

The hills south of Ft. Smith level out for a ways, but start to get steep again about 60 miles south. For the first two days the goin' was easy. On their second night out they camped in the hills again. The people who lived in these hills were not real sociable or friendly. Hunter knew what to expect. They hated strangers and if pressed, would come to gunfights over their presence. Most were armed with old shotguns, so Hunter kept his distance from the tree line if he could.

Tonight they were camped in a creek bed. Close cover all around. They were back to the rabbit and squirrel menu, Hunter didn't mind. They were just pourin' the coffee when Hunter got that little feeling again. He didn't hear anything, but the woods hushed down just a little and he knew they weren't alone. He slowly reached down and laid his finger on the cross draw Colt and waited. They were comin' in he was sure of it.

Donne picked up on what Hunter was doing almost immediately. He had been dry firing the Remington earlier. He slowly started to get cartridges from the belt rolled up in front of him. Hunter shook his head and Donnie stopped.

Hunter said. "If they see that we lose the upper hand. If shootin' starts you make for that shotgun by your bedroll." They waited together, Hunter sipping his coffee, the boy just twitching from the excitement.

About a half hour later two hillbillies walked up from the north. They had circled all the way around the camp and tried to surprise them. It didn't work, Hunter had heard them ten minutes ago and had turned so the cross draw faced them when they came up the trail. He still had a finger lying on the butt of the Colt, coffee in his left hand, kinda layin' on his left side by the fire. Hunter said. "Evenin' Gents" before Donnie could even see them by the firelight. They stopped for a couple seconds then came on in.

One was rail thin and about six foot two. The other was about four and a half feet, tall and wide. The tall one carried an old single shot Springfield left over from the war, Hunter was sure. The other had a rusty ten gauge single shot. It looked older.

The short one said. "Evenin' to you, too I'm John Scott and this is my brother Matthew. We live in a little cabin away up the side of this here mountain. We seen your fire from up there and thought we'd mosey on down here and see if we could help you gentlemens with anything."

"No" Hunter said, "I b'lieve we got everything we need right here boys. Ya'll can just mosey right on back up to that cabin now. We appreciate your concern and all, but we're doin' just fine."

Matthew said, "We could sit a spell and have coffee with you two wanderers."

"Coffee's all gone boys, sorry. Next trip through we'll make a double pot and chew the fat with you boys all evenin' but we got a hard day tomorrow gents and we gotta get some rest."

Matthew started moving a little to his left his hand creeping toward the hammer on the Springfield rifle he was carrying.

Hunter said quietly, "Matthew, If your hand gets any closer to the hammer on that old rifle you'll both be dead before you hear the sear click."

The tall man's hand froze. He looked at Hunter deep in his eyes and decided the stranger layin' by the fire believed what he was saying. More to the point Matthew believed it, too. He said, "Mister we didn't walk all the way down this here mountain to get shot for our trouble. I guess we will just mosey back up to the cabin now and bid you gents a good night." His brother started to protest but Matthew said. "Shut up, John, and head back up the trail."

Hunter and the boy could hear them arguing for a good ways while they hiked back up the hill. When they were out of earshot Hunter looked at Donnie and said, "When a pair like that comes up on you tryin' to make friends while they decide how to rob you, always remember the first one to talk isn't the one who's in charge. He'll always have another talk to you while he sizes you up. When we didn't invite them in for coffee he took over. He ain't stupid. He knew they weren't gunfighters. He also saw in my eyes that I was. They won't bother us again, and the next time I'm through here I'll make a double pot of coffee. Now let's get some sleep." Donnie soaked it all up like a sponge. He adored this man with the terrible hands.

The next morning they started up into the hills. They were rockier and steeper than any hills that Donnie had seen in the Northeast part of the Territories. Hunter said these Arkansawyers and folks from the Territories were the only people with balls enough to call these mountains. They called this little range The Winding Stair Mountains. They were steep enough but Hunter thought whoever named them had never led a pack mule over the Continental Divide. Now THOSE are mountains

After they got up into the hills a day and a half Hunter headed due West on a trail that looked traveled enough. He knew it led to Talehina. Talehina was just a trading post with some Choctaw Indians settling around it. There was trading to be done and the major trail South out of Webber's Falls wound South through Poteau and Talehina. If Lowe was still headed South he'd pass through Talehina. They were still a day away when Hunter said. "This meadow looks like a good place to camp."

It was mid day and Donnie was more than a little surprised.

Hunter said, "Let's clear off a place to build a fire and go huntin'. The deer tracks are thicker than the grass on this trail. The back straps of a young buck sound awful good to me today." They cleared a spot, tied the horses out to graze and left the shotguns with the saddles. They only took the rifle, walking south off the trail through the trees. While they walked, Hunter cut a green branch off a tree and began to trim it down about three feet long with a fork at one end. When it was finished he stuck it in his back pocket.

It only took twenty minutes when Frank touched Donnie's arm and pointed off to their left. He dropped to one knee and the boy did the same as the yearling buck walked past them. He was quartering away from them at about fifty yards. Hunter slowly reached around and grabbed the stick and placed the end on the ground with the fork up. He laid the barrel of the rifle in the fork and took steady aim. At the report of the rifle the buck went down without a quiver. He looked at Donnie, "Always try to make a clean kill on whatever you shoot."

"The back straps are what you'd call the tenderloins on a beef. They are easy to get to and the best part of a deer if you don't have time to stew anything." Hunter said. "The coyotes will clean this up, too." and headed back to camp.

Back at camp Hunter salted and peppered the two slabs of venison and started cooking them slowly, on a flat rock at the edge of the fire in the little skillet. He'd place the pieces on the plate, but kept it close to the fire so the meat wouldn't get cold. While he cooked Donnie dry fired the Remington at a knot in the tree closest to the camp. Hunter thought, "He'll get it, he don't give up easy."

When the meat was finished, Hunter divided the pieces between the plate and the skillet and said, "Let's eat it". And eat they did. Donnie thought it was the best meat he'd ever eaten. After the dishes were rinsed off and stowed and the coffee pot was sittin' on the flat rock Hunter said, "Hand me my saddlebags will ya?" Donnie got them, and Hunter dug in them for the open box of .44-40s. He handed Donnie five of them. He said, "Load 'er up."

As Donnie loaded the pistol Hunter warned him to leave the hammer down on an empty chamber, if he was fond of his feet. Hunter walked out into the woods for a moment and came back with four big pine cones. He tossed them on the ground about twenty feet away. He looked at Donnie and said, "Apart from the war where you shoot men at distance with a rifle from cover;

most of the men I've had to shoot were closer than those pine cones are to you. The reason we shoot at such small targets for practice is, when you're excited and your blood is up, your hands sometimes won't do exactly what your head tells them. We practice small to miss small. If you miss a man's heart, which by the way, is about the size of a pine cone by two inches it's still a lung shot. If you miss it two inches high, it get's his windpipe. If you miss it low, it's a liver shot and he'll bleed out in thirty seconds. If we practiced on man-sized targets and miss them by two inches, you miss him altogether. You understand?"

Donnie nodded that he did and said, "Yes Hunter."

Hunter said, "Ok let's give this a try. What you've been doing around the fire has all been for this. It's gonna be louder than you think. It's not louder than your shotgun, but it's a lot closer to your ears. It's different too, the flash and smoke are right in front of your face, the trick is don't flinch before the shot. You gotta know it's coming and be prepared for it. Flinching after the shot is ok as long as you hit what you are shooting at. Now don't cock the hammer until you are ready to shoot, and don't cock the hammer and stand there and aim for a minute and a half. Bring the weapon to bear; cock the hammer and fire."

Donnie thought about the thousands of dry fires he'd done over the last couple of weeks. He desperately wanted to hit the first pine cone. He raised the pistol, cocked the hammer, and saw the first pine cone right above the front sight. He squeezed the trigger and didn't see the pine cone move off the sight. The bullet hit the ground just beneath the pine cone.

Hunter said, "The front sight is too tall. Make the top of the sight split the target". Donnie pulled up cocked and fired. The pine cone exploded. He repeated three times rapidly, and all four pine cones were gone.

Hunter nodded and said, "I had a suspicion you were gonna be good at this. Now you can get your own pine cones. You have to shoot now until your hand knows where the bullet is going without using the sights. There's thirty left in this box...

Shoot 'em."

Donnie headed off for pine cones.

Hunter headed back to the fire to watch and drink coffee in the late May sun. Donnie shot twenty eight more pine cones. He shot without a miss until the last five shots which he snap shot from waist level... He only hit three of them. Hunter was more than a little surprised. Three out of five after just firing a pistol thirty times, the kid was a natural. Hunter didn't say anything, he just sipped his coffee.

Chapter 11 – The Tellin's the Hard Part Pt. 2

After the sun went down on their afternoon off Hunter sat looking into the fire. Donnie was cleaning the Remington, stopping every few minutes to dry fire it at the knot in the tree. Hunter said almost absently. "I got some more story to tell if ya wanna hear it."

The boy put the gun oil back in the canvas bag and set the pistol aside. He pulled his saddle over across from Hunter and sat down using the saddle for a backrest and said. "I'm all ears." Hunter pulled the pint of bourbon from his pocket and took a little sip, drew a deep breath and started.

"I had a talent for this kind of work all my life. I must have or I'd be dead by now. These outlaws don't have any pause about killin a man. I learned early on that if you were ready to kill them goin' in then you had the upper hand. They had to get ready. Killin' a man is something, I have found, most men have to get ready for. Every time I take a man for bounty I spend a couple of minutes getting' my mind around the thing before I start. If you're ready and he's not, you got the upper hand. Of course a few of them were always ready to do some killin'.

I trailed outlaws all over Texas, Lousiana, Arkansas as far east as Little Rock, up through Kansas as far north as the Platte River in Nebraska.

I was in Dodge City, Kansas after I collected my reward.

The U.S. Marshall there asked me if I would like to be deputized for a while and help him catch a man who had killed a whole family out North of town just for their two saddle horses.

I couldn't abide killin' a family for any reason but, I was in it for the money. I asked the Marshall what it paid. Marshall said. The bounty was one thousand and we could split that. The Gov'ment would outfit us for the trip. So I got deputized, badge and all. Can you imagine it? Frank Hunter Deputy United States Marshall. We lit out after this guy. I seem to recall his name was somethin' Massey...Ryan or Brian? Anyway we lit out after this Massey. The Marshal didn't know which way he went or where he was headed. I had pulled down the wanted poster in the Marshall's office before we left or we wouldn't have even had a picture of the guy. Seems the Marshall was sent out after the guy by the District Judge and didn't know how to trail an outlaw. That's why he wanted my help. At the first town the shopkeeper was sweepin' the plank walkway in front of the dry goods.

I stopped and asked him if he'd seen a fella ridin' a horse and leadin' another through here last week, Wednesday or Thursday.

He thought he remembered that he was headed west like you two. He didn't stop either, came through at a fast gait and kept going.

We just kept goin' West and stoppin' at every cross roads and settlement along the trail and askin' folks if they seen the man on this poster. As we went, I explained the way to do this just like I've been explainin' it to you. Good folks won't abide an outlaw in their midst. A working man has to earn his bread and so should everyone else. The workin' folks are the ones to ask. They'll always help you usually. I kept askin' and they kept pointin' us in the right direction.

An outlaw is a lazy person by nature. If they weren't, they'd have honest jobs. If an outlaw runs enough and gets tired enough he'll talk himself into thinkin' he's given whoever was after him the slip. Nine times out of ten, if you trail a man two weeks you'll catch up to him in the third week. Most lawmen will only trail a man a few days. They have other responsibilities, and so do their posses.

If they can't get out after a bank robber or murderer in a few minutes, they won't catch him. Outlaws are good runners for two weeks. After that they get lazy again. Some will stop and gamble with their loot. Some just go home. I've taken six of the thirty-nine bounties I have collected in their own yards. They ran for two weeks and then went home. Laziness is an outlaw's worst enemy.

We followed this Massey's trail west and north through Colorado. It was early fall and warm in the lower elevations but the higher we got the colder it got.

He got into the hills and went north through Raton and up to Walsenburg. The folks just kept pointin' the way- A general store owner, a liveryman where he'd had a shoe put back on one of the horses. Then at Walsenburg he cut west and up into the mountains proper. Three days up across Wolf Creek Pass we went- me, the Marshal, and an old pack mule with our camp packed on his back. We had bought more blankets and a tent in Walsenburg. Nights were bitter cold up in the Rockies. If you couldn't get out of the wind you'd freeze, even in October.

We came down the other side of the pass and into a little town called Pagosa Springs. We stopped in a saloon to warm up and rest a bit, maybe have a beer and a sandwich. I walked in and sat at a back table facing the door. The Marshall had his back to the ranch hands and the prospectors who's hands were raw and sore from tryin' to pan a little flake out of the San Juan River.

It was a big log buildingwith 4 glass windows on the front. Two of the windows were cracked the batwing doors were new though. Probably got broken throwin' some drunk prospector out through them. It was a fairly new building. The log walls were still seeping pine sap. I knew the logs were still shrinkin' probably why the windows were cracked.

When my eyes fit the light I saw him, in the corner to the

right of the front door. He was alone, just drinkin' good whiskey and watchin' the goingson of the saloon. I closed my eyes for a minute and tried to imagine what would happen next. When the barkeep brought the beers I opened my eyes and told the Marshall to sit tight. I got up and walked toward the front door like I was goin' outside.

When I was right in front of Massey I stopped and turned to him and said, 'Massey, I'm Deputy Marshal Frank Hunter and I'm takin' you in for murderin' a whole family in Dodge City, Kansas for their horses.'

The look on his face was worth the trip over the pass. First, there was shock, thinkin' it had been over three weeks and someone was still following from Kansas. Then, there was fear that he'd been caught and he'd hang in Kansas for this. Then, there was the rage that always took them last as they decide their only option is to kill the man who'd done the following.

Massey grabbed the edge of the table and flipped it up and dropped to his knees behind it. I pulled the old Colt. It was only a year old then. I could hear Massey's pistol cock behind the table. I yelled, 'Don't do it boy,' but, I already knew what would happen. Massey swung the gun around the edge of the table and I put four bullets through the table top- all four of them found Massey on the other side. We packed ol' Massey back up on his horse and headed back up the pass.

He froze solid the first night on the trail. I felt kinda bad because we couldn't give that horse a break without we sawed him in two, to get him off; so he stayed on. When we got back to Walsenburg there was a Marshal's office there and we put in for the reward and slept in beds for a week.

The money came and the Marshal gave me my five-hundred, and I handed him back the badge. He said. 'Hunter why don't you keep it, come back to Dodge and help me keep the peace in that cattle town? Those drovers would have a hard time against the likes of you.'

I said, 'No thanks. I'm good on the trail but the job you

have is too dangerous. I have to be ready at the end of the trail. I follow em for a couple weeks then take em while they're relaxed and sure they're safe. You have to deal with em every day while their blood is up and ready to do some killin'. It's too dangerous for me. I'll just bid you good luck and goodbye right here Marshal.'

I cut South across Eastern Colorado. I crossed the little strip of the Indian Territory that Texas gave them when they entered the War on the side of the Confederacy. They called it the Panhandle, and it looks like one on a map. It was the only part of Texas that was above the Mason-Dixon, so they gave it away. Anyway, I crossed and entered Texas, my home state, and I was still two weeks' ride away from home. Texas is a big Son-of-a-Whore if nothin' else."

Hunter took another sip from the pint. His brow furrowed a bit as he thought of what needed tellin' next. His mind lit on it, and in the firelight Donnie could see the change on Hunter's face.

"Remember when I said folks won't abide an outlaw usually? Well here's the exception to that rule.

When I finally got home from Colorado I stayed at the house for a week or so. When I was gone Marla has a woman come by once a week to sweep, and dust, and air the place out. She has a painter out every couple of years. She's kept it up for me all this time, and I never asked her once to do it; she just does. Anyhow, I went to the Sheriff's office to look at the posters. I came across one for a thousand dollars dead or alive. A young guy named Tommy Lewis, alias Tom Lewis, alias Lazy T. Seems ol' Lazy T had robbed the overland stage up near Hot Springs and killed the driver, and the shotgun rider. He had made off with a currency shipment bound for the bank in Shreveport, forty thousand dollars currency, no gold. He had spared all the passengers on the stage. All of them were able to give a good description, and the picture on the poster was a very detailed one, down to a scar along his left cheek.

I closed up the house and locked the barn. Put some flowers

at Momma's grave and went into town. I pulled up at the Three Doors.

Marla met me at the door and said, 'How about a roast chicken for supper?' I shook my head.

She said, 'You're headed out again aren't you?'

I nodded and she said. 'Why Frank? I get a letter from Anna every week, and Becca has more than everything she needs. You and I don't want for anything right now. Why not just stay at home for a while and live for a change?'

I said, 'Because it's not what I do. I'll go crazy just sittin' around that old place.'

She said, 'Put in a crop for Christ's sake, Frank. You own forty acres out there.'

'It's all growed over, and I ain't made for pullin' stumps or pushin' plows. I love you, but I gotta be gone for a while. This one's close. Be back in a couple of weeks.' I kissed her and told her I loved her, then I walked out. I didn't come back for six weeks.

I got back up in the hills around Hot Springs I stopped at a stage station where they change out the teams, feed the passengers, and get back on the road. I was talkin' with the station man there and asked him how ol' Lazy T knew there was a currency shipment on the stage. The man told me that if there's nothin' in the strongbox, the comp'ny don't pay no shotgun rider. 'He probly just watched the stages until one came along with an ol' boy ridin' shotgun.'

I waited until a stage came through and asked the driver if he'd seen this ol' boy along the road. The driver allowed he had seen the man in the picture along the road two of the last three trips down from St. Louis, seen him around Jessiville.

I lit out for Jessiville, Arkansas. It wasn't far North of Hot Springs. I got there and booked a room at a boarding house. It wasn't big enough for a hotel. I took care of my horse, too. There was no livery, but there was a corral with a lean-to shed to put your saddle in. There was a hay stack in the shed and a box with a slot cut in the top. A sign read. 'Feed yer horse and put him in the corral – 2 bits a day.' I unsaddled him and pitched him a little alfalfa hay from the stack and set out afoot.

First thing I noticed was how no one was workin'; they were all just standin' around. The fact was there was no money to be had. Those folks were huntin' and gardening for everything they ate. They were broke. I went looking for a beer to wet my throat. On the corner of the two main streets was a little clapboard saloon.

There weren't any swingin' doors. The big old wooden doors were open when it was warm and closed when it wasn't. The bar was three thick, oak planks on two old whiskey barrels. The floor was pine planks that had cured out to leave an eighth inch gap between every one. I thought that the kids in this town must buy all their horehound candy with the dimes that roll through the gaps in this floor.

Inside were the barkeep and a piano player and one slightly tattered, extremely pretty, sportin' woman. I sat down at a table and she came over.

She said. 'A whiskey for ya mister?'

I said. 'I'd have a beer if ya got some.'

She informed me that they hadn't had real St. Louis beer in a year now. 'We do have some that Doods makes.'

I asked, 'Doods; what kind of name is that?'

She said, 'I don't know. You want a glass of his brew?'

I said, 'I'll give it a try.'

She left and the barkeep came out from the back with a big earthen crock that he brewed his beer in. She poured me a mug and the head looked good enough, it was a little darker than I was used to but it was cool. They kept the crock in the cellar, and it tasted sweet. I told ol' Doods he could make my beer anytime and I had three while I was there.

The seventy five cents I spent in there must have been all the money Doods had, because he went down the street after I paid up and bought a cigar. I know folks with a vice like tobacco will buy it if they can, and Doods didn't have a cigar until I had paid for my beer.

While I sipped the last beer the woman came back over and said. 'Mister if you have two dollars we could go in the back and have a good time for a while before the evening rush.'

I said. 'The rush, You kiddin', ain't you?'

She said she just didn't want me thinkin' nothin' was happenin' here and leaving. She said we could go back for a dollar.

I asked her name, she said it was Sarah. I told her. 'Sarah, if you sit here and look pretty while I drink this last beer I'll give you a dollar for your time.'

She smiled and sat next to me and looked beautiful. I gave her two. I told her I might be back for more beer. I might also want to go back for that fun she was talkin about.

She smiled and said 'You won't be sorry.'

I asked her, as I walked out, if she had seen this guy in the picture. She said she'd never seen him in her life. The pretty smile had changed. It was forced and not natural. I knew she was lying.

Over the next two days I asked twenty people if they had seen the guy in the picture, and no one knew him. I went back to the saloon to get some more of that sweet brew...and maybe some fun in the back room. I was sitting there when I realized something. As I looked around the saloon, that was busy compared to my first visit; I realized they were all wearing new shoes, every one of them. I paid my tab and walked around town a bit and every person I saw had on brand new shoes. This was Lazy T's home town and it was so poor he had robbed the stage for food and shoes for this little town. I thought "Who can I get to tell me where he is? I'm sure by now he knows I'm here for him." I smiled when it occurred to me. I walked up and down the street till I saw the sign I was looking for. It was small, hanging over a shop behind a little frame house.

It simply said COBBLER. If anyone would tell me where he was it was the man who wasn't fixing any shoes right now.

I walked into the cobbler's shop and said. 'I need a half sole on these boots but, they're the only boots I have.'

The cobbler said. 'I can do that while you wait if you have a half hour.'

I told him I did. He set about cutting the new leather soles as I sat there in my sock feet. I said, 'It's lucky your business is slow today, I'd walk right out of those old boots.'

He allowed the soles needed done but weren't that bad yet. Besides he had no other customers anyway.

I looked puzzled and asked why he had no customers. 'Usually hard times mean good business for repairmen of all trades, cheaper to fix than replace.'

He said. 'Everyone in town bought new shoes.'

I said. 'Did they now? How'd it come to pass that everyone got money all at once?'

The cobbler looked at me flatly and said. 'Mister I know who you are and why you're here and who you're lookin' for. I told Doods to tell everyone to put their old shoes on. He didn't think you'd notice. You are smarter than they give you credit for Mister.'

I nodded my agreement.

'I can't tell you where he is. He's kinda saved this little town from starvin' this comin' winter.'

I said, 'Looks to me like what he's done is saved them, and screwed you. Did you know he killed the driver and the shotgun rider on that stage?'

The cobbler shook his head. Apparently Lazy T had left that part out.

I told him, 'I will eventually find him. I am a patient man and I never give up.'

That night Sarah came to the boarding house and washed my back in the tub. Then I returned the favor. Next morning, as she was leaving she asked me about the new soles on my boots.

I told her I had to have them done, but that was alright. I

had a nice long talk with the cobbler.

She said, "Oh that's nice. Frank I gotta get to work."

I said, "See you around kid." She hurried out the door. I watched out the window as she went into the saloon and about thirty seconds later Doods came out and headed for the cobbler's shop. He was in there about ten minutes. I was downstairs havin' coffee and biscuits when Doods came in and sat down at my table.

He looked across at me and said. "Mister Hunter, Why don't you just go home and let us be?"

I said, "I ain't doin' a thing to you folks except spend a little money in this shit-hole of a town that, by the way, looks like it needs it."

Doods asked. "What is the reward on Tommy anyway?"

I told him it was a thousand dollars. "He shouldn't have killed the driver and the guard."

Doods nodded his agreement. Then he asked the question I knew I was going to hear. I've heard it from a lot of the guys who steal a lot of money. Doods said, "What if I gave you the thousand would you just go away?"

I took my time chewing the damned dry biscuit and washing it down with pretty good coffee before I said. "Doods, I just can't do that. I know you think a bounty hunter will do anything for money but, that's just not the case here. He killed two men who were just trying to make their living and he needs to answer for it. I'm gonna bring him into Hot Springs, dead or alive. It's up to him."

Doods said, "Everyone here owes him their life. You *might* not live to take him in Mr. Hunter."

I looked at him and said, "Well Doods, I heard *mites* grow on a chicken's ass." His face turned red and he got up and stomped out.

They tried over the next two weeks to get me to leave. Every day I'd get up and walk up and pitch some hay to my horse, make sure the water trough was full and put two bits in the box.

I'd walk down to the saloon and buy two beers. Somewhere along the way they got some real beer. I missed Doods' home brew. I killed some time with Sarah. She was trapped here and none of it was her fault. They were getting' nervous and I knew it would be soon.

After I'd been there three weeks I was headed back to the boarding house just after supper. The days were getting short and it was almost dark. Two boys I had seen in the saloon came from behind the saloon as I cleared the alley. Both had shotguns both of them were cocked.

I said. "Think about it, boys, you'll be murderers. The next bounty hunter in town will be lookin' for you".

That slowed them down long enough. I rolled to my left pulling the Colt as I rolled. I fanned the hammer four times and hit them both in the chest twice. I reloaded. Never know when someone else would try again. They didn't. I stood in the street, knowing the whole town was watching and yelled. "He's killed four now!" I went to bed.

The next morning at breakfast I was tryin' to choke down those damned biscuits when a stocky man about five-ten came in and sat across from me. He had a scar on his cheek and he looked sad.

He said. "Mister, my name's Tom Lewis. Some call me Lazy T. That don't matter, though, what matters is my two cousins you killed in the street last night. They were just doin' what I told em to do".

I said. "I know they were. The fact of the matter is, and I want you to listen close, Tommy; you killed those boys as sure as if you pulled the trigger yourself. I am not gonna get shot down from ambush just because they were doin' what you told them to do". I went on and said. "Now, I came here Tommy to take you into Hot Springs for the robbery of the Overland Stage, and the murderin' of the driver and guard. Will you come quiet? I know you were just feedin' these folks here, but you can't sidestep the murders."

He looked like he was gonna come then he said. "They shot first, it was them or me. I know it was wrong, it just couldn't be helped. Now, Mr. Hunter I got a .32 Derringer pointed at yer gut. I'm gonna back out of here. My brother, Lonnie has a rifle outside. If you come out the door in the next five minutes he'll kill you like you did my cousins. I'm just gonna fade back into them hills and oblige you to come get me sir."

He stood up and be damned if he didn't really have a Derringer.

I said. "I need to finish my breakfast first. Then I'll be out. Tell ol' Lonnie to be ready, see if you can go for five killed because of you". He backed out the door. I knew he'd be easy to find. He felt bad about what happened. He just didn't have the guts to swing for it. I didn't blame him either. I'd fight an army to stay out of the hangman's noose.

I finished my biscuits and had another half cup of coffee. I went outside. I guess Lonnie had enough of waiting for me 'cause I didn't see anything out of place. I walked up the hill and led my horse out of the corral and saddled him up for the first time in two weeks. I rode out of town to the north about three miles. I was thinkin' that Lazy T and ol' Lonnie would be waitin' around every bend in the road but they weren't. I headed back to town and went out south then east and west, not a sign of him. I tied my horse up at the saloon. I walked back up the street. I had a cobbler to talk to.

I usually don't resort to paying for information. Like I said, usually folks will offer that up to get rid of an outlaw, not this time. I walked into the cobbler's shop. The little brass bell above the door jingled my entrance. The cobbler was sittin there drinkin' whiskey at one in the afternoon. He wasn't tanked but he was on his way.

I said to him. "I know everyone here knows I came down here. I am only gonna offer this once and I understand if you turn me down flat. I will pay you one hundred dollars gold if you point me to where Lazy T is. I know he's put you out of work for a year. I also noticed you don't have on new shoes. I expect your pantry has flour and beans from the money he took.

The money he took is gone. I don't care about that. I just want Tommy. He's gonna pay for the driver and shotgun rider. If he goes in he'll hang in Hot Springs. From my past experience he will make me kill him. Most men would rather fight with a gun than go in to swing and I understand that. He needs to know that others will come after me so killin' me won't solve it. It will just postpone it." I looked at him and waited. I could see he was givin' it a good amount of thought.

After a couple of minutes he looked at me and said. "If I tell you, you gotta look out south of town for a few days." I nodded, I understood he had to live here and these folks might take revenge on him if they thought he helped me. "Next" he said, "I'll need to see the money."

I took off my hat and counted out five gold coins. He looked at it like it was a fortune. He'd been too broke too long to pass this up. He told me and looked relieved. Lazy T's shack was four miles north of town about a mile and a half up in the hills east of the main road.

The next day I rode out south after breakfast. I took a good look around in case anyone was watching. I let everyone think the cobbler didn't tell me a thing. I shot a rabbit for supper and built a fire. I got back into town around dark.

I went to the saloon for a beer after I put my horse away. Sarah asked if I needed my back washed tonight. I told her it didn't sound like a bad idea. She showed up around eight o'clock. She stayed the night.

The next morning I rode out east with an idea I'd see something to throw me off. I wasn't wrong. About three miles east of town I saw something shiny about a hundred yards off to my left. It was the overland strong box from the stage. It had three bullet holes around the lock. Apparently ol' Lazy T was a bad shot to top it off. There were still dried blood stains on it from the shotgun rider. If this box had been outside all this time the stains would have been washed off by the weather. It was planted here recently to keep me in this area. I decided to give Tommy one more day. I'd come back out here tomorrow. Tonight I'd spread it around that I found a lead in the woods.

I did just that. Everyone in the saloon looked pleased that I'd found something. They were pleased their decoy was working. I spent the next day napping in the woods I ate two of the hard biscuits I had gotten from the boarding house. They were as bad in the afternoon as they were in the morning. I went in early.

On the last day I was in Jessiville, Arkansas I went north. I just walked my horse along watchin' the road. I saw the place where Tommy was making the left turn off the road. I had the feelin' so I went on by. About a mile past Lazy T's place I turned east up into the woods. I tied my horse off on an old blackjack tree and sat down and waited. If I wasn't wrong he'd be along in a minute trying to shadow me on the road. I loaded the empty chamber on the colt. I sat there with my back against the blackjack tree and it took five minutes for Tommy to come over the ridge.

When he saw me he was 50 yards to my two o'clock. I sat there waiting to see if he'd pull up the rifle. If he did I'd have to take cover for a good shot. I didn't have the Winchester yet. I had the Greener on the saddle, but it was next to useless at this range.

He walked on in and stood there lookin' at me and said. "Well you found me, now what?"

I told him I was here to take him back to the Marshall in Hot Springs for the robbery of the Overland Stage and the murders of the driver and guard.

He said. "I know that. I meant how are you gonna do it.

I said. "If you come peaceably and don't talk too much I'll give you over to the Marshall and he'll have a trial when the Judge comes back to town. Then they'll give you a proper hangin' at the gov'ments expense."

He asked. "What about the money?"

I told him the money didn't figure into if as far as I was concerned. I was just here for him. The stage company put up the thousand for the reward and that's all I was interested in.

He said. "Well in that case I'm tired of hidin' out in these hills. I think I'm either gonna kill you or you're gonna kill me right now."

I asked him, "Do you have a horse here?"

He said, "I do indeed, back at the cabin. Why?"

I told him I'd need something to haul him back into Hot Springs on.

He thumb cocked that old rifle and hip shot. The bullet went into and out of my left shoulder. It was a single shot rifle he was reloading as I drew the Colt.

I said, "You can still stop."

He pulled the lever up and started to cock the hammer when I shot him in the forehead. He lurched a couple of times and then went down.

I reloaded and checked my shoulder. It went clean through it needed cleaning but all I could tell was, it was gonna be sore. I rode up to Tommy's cabin and saddled his horse. I went back as fast as I could and got him on before my shoulder stiffened up. I tied him under the horse and around his middle to the saddle horn and headed back to Jessiville. I left ol' Lazy T hangin there in front of the boarding house while I cleaned my shoulder and packed my things. I stopped at the desk and settled up including two extra dollars for the pillowcases I made the bandage and sling out of. I walked outside to a crowd of six or seven folks who just looked heartbroken. They stood around my horse looking like it was their momma draped over the saddle, Doods was one of them.

He asked if they could give him a decent burial.

I told him if one of them followed me into Hot Springs I was sure the Marshall would release the body to them after the identification was over.

He said, "Then I'll ride along with you Mr. Hunter if you

don't mind".

I allowed I didn't. He didn't talk much, which was good.

In Hot Springs the Marshal looked at him for about thirty seconds and said, "That's him, I'll put in for your reward tomorrow. Be here to sign the forms at ten in the morning."

I said, "This man's his friend. Can he take him home and bury him?"

"Sure", the Marshall said, "save the county ten bucks."

Doods took Lazy T's horse by the reins and headed back to Jessiville. I waited five days for my money and headed back to Texarkana.

Marla was none too happy about my two weeks stretchin' into six but she didn't bitch much. She got to nurse me and I wasn't leaving for a while. That shoulder hurt like a Son-of-a-Whore. I'd been nicked a few time in the war and such but this was my first honest to God bullet wound. First it burned and hurt, then it itched all the way through my shoulder, deep inside where you couldn't scratch. The muscle hurt when I moved it but Marla made me move it as soon as I could without tearin' the wound open. Half an hour a day I raised my arm and lowered it. It felt like it was filled with crushed glass. I lived through it and it was because of Marla. I'd be crippled today if she hadn't pushed me. I stayed home six months.

The winter's the best time to stay home if you're goin' to. I paid an old man to haul me fire wood and stayed indoors when it was cold. I rode into town when it wasn't and had a beer at the Three Doors. I shot a couple of nice bucks and made jerky after I roasted the back straps. In general I mended all that winter. I had a roof over my head and three meals if I wanted them. I had Marla almost every night. She'd work till dark waitin' tables and goin upstairs with the occasional cowboy or card player. Then she's come out to the house. Thinkin' back now it was the best winter of my life.

When May rolled around and I could feel the warmth in the air I started to get a little stir crazy. My shoulder was mended. I could lift as much as I ever could. It just kinda ached sometimes. It still does when it's cold. I saddled up and went to the Sheriff's office to look at the posters. I found one, it was for twelve hundred, dead or alive. Larry (Lucky) Curtis wanted for murdering his wife and her lover. I pulled the poster down and headed back to the house. I packed my saddlebags, coffee, coffee pot, skillet, fork, cup, the rest of the deer jerky, bed roll, and the little canvas bag that held my solvent, oils, and brushes to clean my tools. I headed into town I stopped at the bank and made a withdrawal. I stopped at the general store and bought that ol' '73 Winchester and scabbard, and then I went to the Three Doors.

Marla was sittin' on the piano, her skirts up over her knees, singin' The yellow Rose of Texas at the top of her lungs. There were half a dozen cowboys puttin' dollars in her garters and tryin' to get a peek up a little higher. When she saw me she knew I was headed out. I guess she could read my face. She stopped singin' and hopped down. She said. "I'll be right back boys." She walked out the batwing doors on the east side of the saloon. There were batwings on the north and south sides too. Outside she said. "Frank, be careful and don't get shot this time. When you're out there remember you have a home here. We could get along fine if you stayed."

I told her that this was the only thing I was good at.

She said. "I don't believe that; it's just the only thing you've found so far. I love you Frank Hunter."

I said "I love you too Baby-Doll. I mounted up and rode out for Tyler, Texas. I figured he was headed for the Territories. I wasn't wrong.

It's been the same shit in my life for the last nineteen years. I go after someone, catch them, sometimes I go home, sometimes I go out after another. It all depends where I put in for the reward and the time of year. Damn it's getting' late. We'd better turn in, we'll shoot some more in a couple of days. You keep dry firing that Remington in the evenings."

Chapter 12 – Tracking a Horse

The next morning they set out for Talehina. When they got there, they went to the general store and showed the poster around. The owner said he hadn't seen the man in the picture, but the stock boy had. Hunter could see the recognition in his eyes. Hunter asked him if he'd seen this man. The boy looked to the shopkeeper for permission to speak.

The owner said. "Well boy, you seen him or not"?

The kid who was about fourteen said he had seen him about a week ago." He came in while you were at lunch sir. Remember the fifty dollar bill"?

The shop keeper said. "Oh that was the man eh? I came back from lunch and the boy here had made a sale of ten dollars worth of jerky and a box of shells and got paid with a fifty. Wiped out all the change I had. Had to ride over to Poteau and get some fives and ones."

Hunter asked. "Son, did you see which way he went from here?"

The boy allowed he rode out south on the main road.

Hunter said thanks to the boy then bought another box of .44-40s to replace the box that got shot up yesterday. They left out south on the main road. He was a week behind just like he had started this hunt. He had gained a shotgun, a partner, and nine hundred dollars since he started, but he was still a week behind. Hunter also knew that if they chased him another week he'd stop and rest. He'd get lazy, they always did.

Hunter told Donnie. "We'll try to gain a day on him by ridin' hard and late every day. Along about an hour before sundown get your shotgun out and try to shoot supper from your horse. We'll ride till dark or maybe a little longer if the moon's good and the terrains not too steep".

Donnie shot a fine pair of squirrels for their supper. It was gettin' hot, today was the first day Hunter took the Sheriff's Colt out of his sleeve and rolled his coat up and tied it to the saddle with his bedroll. They'd cook up the squirrels and hit the sack as early as they could.

After last night Donnie thought he'd have no problem. Donnie thought about Hunter's story as he followed the man up the trail. He thought about how an outlaw is lazy and will run a while then stop. He also thought about the man Lazy T who was just tryin' to keep his people from starving. If he hadn't killed the two guys Donnie thought, Hunter would have let him go; at least he liked to think he would have. If the time got right he'd ask him.

They stopped an hour after the last of the sun was gone behind the hills; still light enough to find firewood. Donnie skinned squirrels; hunter started the fire and the coffee.

Squirrels are a lot harder to skin than a rabbit. Rabbit skin really just falls off when you get the edges open, not a squirrel's though. You gotta get an edge up and pull like hell to get it loose. It's more like skinning an ol' catfish Donnie was thinkin' when Hunter asked him why he'd been so quiet this evenin'.

He said. "I been doin' some thinkin' is all. About the stories you told me last night and about the way we're chasin' ol' David Lowe 'cause we know he'll get lazy and stop again, and why squirrel skin can't just fall off like a rabbit's.

Hunter looked at him a moment and asked. "Did ya come up with anything for all that thinkin"?

Donnie paused and said. "Yep, I decided since they're all rats anyway, I'll try to shoot more rabbits". They both smiled. As far as Donnie knew it was the first smile he'd seen on Hunter since they'd met. He hadn't seen Hunter when he smiled. Frank liked to keep the smiles to himself.

The next Morning they had coffee, broke camp and were ridin' for an hour before the sun came up. They were about three hours down the trail when hunter reigned the big gelding up and said, "Let's look at this a minute". Off to the side of the road, which was two wagon ruts with bluestem grass growing between the ruts, was a cold campfire and some trash left behind. The trash was the paper bag from the jerky he bought in Talehina. It still smelled of old venison and smoke. Around the fire Hunter looked in the bushes for a track the wind hadn't blown away. He found one, left rear hoof, three nails on the left, two nails on the right. It was Lowe's camp. It wasn't a week old either, four or five nights as close as Hunter could tell.

They left the camp and stayed on the trail till well after dark. Donnie shot a fat cottontail on the trail. It skinned so much easier. They cooked fast and turned in.

Hunter awoke in the night the fire was just embers. It was gettin' late in June and it wasn't cold. He didn't need the fire for the chill, he just wanted the light. He put a couple of small sticks in the embers and soon they flared up. He guessed it at two in the morning. Hunter never carried a watch. He'd had plenty of money to buy one. He'd even killed several men who carried watches he could have kept for himself. He just didn't want to be that way. When he was in the army everything was timed to the minute - when they slept, when they woke, when they ate. After he left Nashville his watch stopped working on the way back to Texarkana. Hunter wound it and it still wouldn't run. He threw it into the bushes along the road and never needed one since.

He laid there awake for an hour or so thinking about Lowe's frame of mind. He imagined David Lowe riding along ahead of them thinking. "Those bounty hunters got ol' Big Jim. When they collect their money they'll go to Ft. Smith. He was big stuff, they'll drink in Ft. Smith a while. I should be out of their minds by now." That's why he was travelin' so slow. He was sure again that no one was following him. He didn't know Frank Hunter. He'd given up on exactly one bounty since he started this. Every other poster he'd pulled down he'd brought in. He didn't give up on a bounty.

Hunter dozed a little before dawn. He started the coffee and dozed a little more. Donnie woke him pourin' coffee into the cups. Hunter said. "Mornin' kid, if we find another fire a little fresher today we'll take 'er a littler easier tonight. I don't wanna catch him in these hills. Up here it's too easy for him to slip into the brush if he hears us coming. We'll wait till he lights, then we'll take him."

They came to a stream and stopped to water the horses. Hunter filled his canteen and Donnie was drinking from his cupped hands. Donnie stood up and asked Hunter if he could strap on that Remington and dry fire at the rocks in the road. Hunter allowed that should be alright, since they had ridden too late the last two nights to practice. Hunter said if anyone comes along to start trouble you throw that thing on the ground. Is that clear? Donnie nodded. Hunter said. "Say it."

Donnie said. "I will throw it down if someone comes and starts trouble."

Donnie walked around his little paint and rummaged around in the saddlebag. He came out with the belt that Hunter had modified for him. It was a good thing hunter left some growin' room in it. He already had to use the next bigger notch in the belt. Even just eatin' once a day it was more than ol' Preston used to feed him. He'd put on around ten pounds, probly put on five in Ft. Smith. He buckled it on and tied the leather thong around his thigh. It had a satisfying creak when he walked and a satisfying heft to it. It felt natural to Donnie to have it there. He clicked the loading gate open and spun the cylinder to see it wasn't loaded. He got another drink then he mounted up.

Hunter rode on up the trail and listened to Donnie behind him. He tried to gauge the time between the slap of the boy's palm against the walnut grip on the revolver and the click of the hammer falling on an empty chamber. He judged it at roughly a half a second. Not as fast as Hunter but damned fast, especially for a kid. Hunter wondered as he rode along if he'd done the kid a dis-service by introducing him to the tools of his trade. They could get him killed. Hunter didn't want to think about that happening. He already knew the kid was not squeamish about the killin'. His original plan to get him on at a ranch seemed like it might not happen. It was lookin' more and more like Hunter was trainin' a partner. What the hell, the boy could very well make a good partner. It was true that he helped out on the trail. On the other hand Hunter had gotten along on the trail a long time without a partner. The Marshal in Dodge being the only other time he'd partnered up, and the Marshal just sat and drank beer while Hunter took Massey for the bounty. The kid, Hunter believed, would stand his ground and take the bounty if he was trained. They needed to find the boy a rifle.

Around noon they found the campfire. It was cold but still fresh enough the embers were still all in place. "That's a two day old fire." Hunter said. "See how you can still see the shape of the sticks of wood in the embers? If it was older they would have fallen apart. The little breezes even in these woods will blow the embers apart. Up on the hill the embers won't last as long. The wind's stronger up there. Now, look at this track. See the nail heads in the track? Three on the left and two on the right, that's the same track that was in Lowe's stall at the livery in Webber's Falls. It's his fire alright and we're two days behind him. He's sure we went to Ft. Smith to drink up our bounty for Big Jim and no one's after him. We have the advantage on him again. He's as lazy as the rest of them. They can talk themselves into believing what comforts them."

That night they camped a couple of hours before dark and, hunted up a rabbit and some polk along the trail. The greens went well with the rabbit. They needed another pan if they were gonna keep this up. Hunter gave Donnie fifteen shells and told him to shoot five from the hip at a rock against the side of the bluff. He drew slowly and squeezed the trigger. The sandstone rock exploded. Hunter said. "OK, now draw as fast as I heard you drawing on the trail today." Donnie holstered the pistol and Hunter said to him. "Now listen, it's easy to squeeze one off down your leg if you're not careful. I pull the hammer back with my thumb while I'm drawing the gun but don't put my finger on the trigger until the muzzle is pointed down range. That keeps me from shootin' myself in the knee."

Donnie shook out his hands and drew. Hunter was right, it was about a half second and a big chunk of the original rock exploded as well. Hunter said you practice that till the rest of those shell are gone. Hunter sat down against his saddle and watched as the boys hands learned what would probably be the trade he would practice till an outlaw got him first.

After it was full dark, Hunter walked to the top of the bluff and looked out at the valley below. On the rim of the valley some fifteen or twenty miles to the southeast Hunter thought he saw the twinkle of a camp fire. Donnie had built their fire down below the bluff to keep that damned south wind from blowing their fire away, so it was out of sight. Hunter didn't want Lowe to know anyone else was in this country.

Chapter 13 – Broken Bow

The next morning dawned bright and sultry. The long dog days of summer were coming. This was just a hint of what was just around the corner. July and August were real scorchers around here. It would be as hot as West Texas and as humid as Baton Rouge, the worst of both worlds Hunter thought to himself. He rolled his jacket up first thing and tied it up with his bedroll. Hunter finished his coffee and said; "You might as well load that Remington and strap it on. Here are the rules. If we get in a scrape you don't start anything till I do. You don't have a chip on your shoulder about anything. You never wear it into a saloon unless we're taking a bounty or just havin' a beer, nothing stronger. Talented hands and whiskey don't mix. Someone taught me that long ago. If you don't feel ready, don't wear it. It's not mandatory."

Donnie fairly yelled. "I'm ready Hunter, I think I'm good at this."

Hunter said. "You do have good hands but you're head has to be in the right place. I think your hands are ready, but is your head?"

"It is," Donnie insisted and strapped the belt on. He moved the hunting knife that Hunter had given him to the gun belt. He got five shells from his belt and loaded the Remington, put it in the holster and put the leather loop over the hammer spur to keep it in place if a limb scraped it or something.

He mounted up and looked at Hunter who had been putting the coffee pot away. He said. "Ready?" Hunter just mounted up and headed out.

They covered about half of the valley before noon when they met an old man on a mule leading another mule headed north. They stopped to ask him if he'd met this fella in the picture along the road.

He said. "Sure did, yesterday evenin', he was makin' camp on the far rim of the valley. He didn't want to trade for anything 'cept a jug o' whiskey. He give me ten dollars for a jug of rot-gut rye I bought in Broken Bow. He needed it wors'n I did. I just give two for it."

Hunter asked, "What else you got on that mule. I'm lookin' for a rifle if you got a '73 Winchester."

The old man allowed he had three rifles on the mule. He said. It'll take me a bit to get 'em unpacked.

Hunter replied. "We got time mister. I was thinkin about buildin' a fire for coffee if you want a cup." He said he'd love one, so Donnie gathered sticks while Hunter shaved some kindlin'. They had coffee on in just a few minutes.

The old trader had the rifles out about the time Hunter was pourin coffee. He said. "Mister, we only have two cups. Do you have a third?" He did and handed it over, Hunter filled it and they all three stood there a minute and sipped coffee in the shade of a tall cottonwood.

Then the old man asked. "Whatcha think of those rifles."

Hunter said. "Ask the kid, he's buyin' today not me."

Donnie walked around to look at the rifles and saw the one he wanted right away. There was a Sharps Carbine in .45-70, a Model 73 Winchester carbine, and a '73 Winchester rifle with a 30 inch octagonal barrel. It had a full length magazine and it was brand new. It still smelled like oil. Donnie asked. "How much for this one?"

The old man scratched his head and said. "Well since you made the coffee I could let you have it for fifty five dollars."

Hunter knew the old man had bought it in Broken Bow for forty but he let the kid make his own deal. Besides if the kid wanted it he had plenty of money. He just didn't know if the boy remembered he had it.

Hunter said. "Look and see what the caliber it is." He knew .44-40 was the caliber most of the '73s were.

Donnie read the barrel and said it was a .44-40. Donnie looked at the trader and said. "You got a scabbard for this rifle on that mule"?

The old man rummaged around in one of the baskets and came out with a pretty good lookin' scabbard and a box of shells. He said. "Sixty for the lot."

Donnie looked tortured and then he remembered the money he'd wired to Texarkana and smiled. He said. "Done" He took off his hat and pulled three twenty dollar gold pieces out from behind the hat band. He handed them over to the old man and thanked him.

The old man and Hunter talked about Lowe and which way he was headed as Donnie loaded the Winchester. Damned thing held fifteen rounds in the magazine. He tied the scabbard onto his saddle on the right hand side with the shotgun in the rawhide laces that held the scabbard. He could get to either easily. He would clean it tonight, weather it needed it or not. After a bit they headed out. The old man was packin' his mule back up. As they rode off Donnie asked. "Hunter, Did I pay him too much for this rifle"?

Hunter answered his question with a question. "Do you like it more than those three gold pieces ridin' around in your hat?"

Donnie said. "I sure do, it's a beauty ain't it hunter".

Hunter said. "They're all pretty when they're new. I was

glad to see you didn't choose the carbine. The sight plane is shorter and they only hold ten shells. If you get pinned down by some raiding Commanches that are all pissed off about something the Gov'ment promised them, and crawfished on, you'll be glad for those five extra shots. I think you made a damned good buy. It's something you needed; the price was fair. The old man made a few dollars, and you have what I think is the finest repeating rifle in the world".

That night they built their fire on top of Lowe's embers. They were still warm when they got there. He was still a full day ahead of them and they were two days maybe three out of Broken Bow. Donnie slept with that rifle beside him on the blanket, and the Remington hangin' on his saddle horn next to his head.

Tomorrow hunter would teach marksmanship to Donnie. It was different than shootin' a pistol. Shootin' a pistol was a reflex thing. Either you could do it or you couldn't. Rifle marksmanship was a skill not a talent. Hunter could, given enough time, teach marksmanship to a blue tick hound.

In the morning after coffee and packin' up, Hunter picked up a piece of the deadfall wood that was left from the fire. He mounted up and rode about a hundred yards back up the trail. He looked to make sure no one was coming up the road and stood the stick up in the road. He rummaged around in his saddlebag and found a box of shells that only had a few left in it. He pushed the shells into his belt and hung the box on the stick. He rode back to where Donnie was and said. "A rifle is a hunting or defensive weapon. It's made to shoot at something from distance. This rifle will, when you get it sighted in, shoot the gnats off a dog's pecker at a hundred yards. At a hundred and fifty you'll be lucky to hit the dog. A .44-40 runs out of steam at a hundred yards. Now get down on your belly and rest your elbows on the ground, jack a round into the chamber, line up those sights at the box and squeeze the trigger. Concentrate on your breathing. Don't hold your breath. Draw in a long breath let it out and squeeze."

Donnie lay flat out on his belly, worked the lever on the new Winchester, took careful aim and… The bullet hit the ground a foot in front of the stick. Hunter told him to push the stepped ramp into the rear sight two notches and try again. Donnie did as he was bid only this time he pulled the shot. Hunter saw what he did and told him to try again and squeeze the trigger slowly. It should be a surprise to you when the shot goes off.

Donnie did it again and this time he squeezed the trigger slowly and the bullet nicked the stick about 2 inches below the box. Hunter said "One more notch on that sight, it'll probly be an inch too high so aim at the top edge of the box." Donnie hit the box dead center. Three more shots produced the same result. Hunter said. "Load the thing back up and let's get going". Donnie reloaded the rifle from the box in his saddle bag and slid the Winchester into the scabbard. They saddled up and rode southeast along the road that wound around the hills south to Broken Bow. They were headed for trouble.

That night Donnie cleaned the Winchester, reloaded it and leaned it up against a tree with his shotgun next to his saddle. After the two rabbits were gone, the dishes rinsed and packed and, the coffee drank they bedded down. Hunter was just dozing off when the hairs on the back of his neck stood up. He said. "Boy, cock that shotgun and when it starts don't shoot me. I'll be movin' but there's enough moon to see by. Jack a round into that Winchester and use it after the shotgun's empty."

Donnie asked. "More thieves?"

Hunter just said. "Indians."

The fire being out helped them. The Cherokees came from both directions at once Donnie waited until the first got within twenty yards of their fire before he gave him a gut-full of buck shot. The second to show himself came from behind them and hunter shot him in the head with the old Colt. The rest came at once from both directions two from Donnies end and three from hunters. They came firing Winchesters and whooping at the top of their lungs. Hunter fanned the hammer and turned to see Donnie Fire the second barrel of the shotgun as a bullet tore through his saddle just inches from his head. He dropped the scattergun and grabbed up his new rifle and sent a .44 caliber slug out to greet their last guest. Seven of them, they weren't a violent people as a rule but Hunter knew what they were capable of if they were in the jug and had the numbers on you. "Prob'ly smelled the fire and thought they'd kill us for the horses". Hunter said. "In the mornin' we'll pick up their rifles and leave em here." Hunter heard their horses in the night. Tied up at least a half-mile away, he'd go turn 'em loose in the morning.

He sat down and started another pot of coffee and started to reload his pistols when he saw his Greener leaning against the tree where he'd left it. A stray bullet had sheared off the left hand hammer near the screw that attached it. The Greener had been a gift from Marla and he treasured it more than anything he owned. It was a fine walnut piece of furniture with business on the other end.

He picked up the greener and unloaded the left barrel. He looked it over and, the rest of the English shotgun was basically untouched. He'd find a gunsmith in Broken Bow to fix it.

In the morning after coffee they picked up the rifles and bundled them onto the back of Donnie's paint. They tied them off with some rawhide and went to find their horses. Hunter was right, up the hill to the east were seven ponies tied to tree limbs. Hunter unbridled them one at a time and slapped their butts. There was a pile of hand tied leather bridles and blankets. It was summer or Hunter would have kept the blankets. He did keep some of the leather bridle though. "Can't have too much tie down material"he said. He made a couple more ties on the bundle of rifles. There were three decent Winchesters and Four old Henrys, worn but serviceable. Who knows Donnie might get his sixty bucks back in Broken Bow. They could for sure if they'd sell the Indian scalps, but Hunter wouldn't do it, and wouldn't allow anyone else to either.

They left for Broken Bow. It'd be tomorrow before they got there. Lowe would probly be there this morning. He might be lookin' down on it right now.

About mid day hunter raised a hand to stop Donnie. He dismounted and kneeled in the road. Hunter had been seein' Lowe's tracks in the road all morning. He really didn't need to track him yet. He knew where he was goin' next. He just tracked him to keep sharp. Hunter said. "Lowes horse lost his shoe. He lost the one I been trackin'. He'll hit the blacksmith in Broken Bow." Hunter walked back along the trail about forty yards. He bent and picked up the shoe. You could see the clean spots where the nail heads have been, and the dirt filled hole where the one nail had been missing. He tossed the horseshoe into the weeds and mounted back up. He said. "In Broken Bow we have a lead. Bernie Freeman's the blacksmith there. I've known him for years. If Lowe stopped to get his horse shod Bernie will know everything there is to know about him. He's just kinda easy to talk to, and he don't forget much."

They camped that night and built a fire on top of Lowe's ashes. They were on the south face of a big hill and after dark they could see the twinkling of the lanterns in Broken Bow in the distance. Hunter said. "Prob'ly still twenty miles off, we won't catch him there. I think he's headed back to Texas where I started chasing him. He's beat a path south since Webber's Falls. Not too fast but steady south without wandering. He has a destination in mind and I can't believe it's in these hills. He's goin' back to Texas alright."

They broke camp early the next morning - fast coffee and loaded up and gone. They rode into Broken Bow around noon. It was hot and muggy in these hills. Hunter couldn't wait to get out in the open where the breeze could blow. They reigned up at the livery/blacksmith shop. The sign said BF Livery and Blacksmith. Bernard Freeman Proprietor. Hunter dismounted and stepped into the shade inside the barn.

Out of the back stepped a small but not frail man of about

fifty five. He looked at Hunter a moment and said. "How ya doin' Frank?"

Frank replied. "Pretty fair Bernie, pretty fair." Hunter told Bernie he wanted to give these two horses some grain. "They been grazin' in them hills a week and they need some energy to take 'em on in."

Bernie went about puttin the horses in stalls while Hunter unfolded the poster he'd pulled down in Wichita Falls. He asked Bernie if he'd seen this fella yesterday.

Bernie nodded.

Hunter waited a few seconds and then said, "Well, are ya gonna tell me about him or not?"

Bernie smiled at Donnie and said. "Oh, you wanna know about him. You just asked if I'd seen him, not if I knew anything about him."

Hunter said. "I know better than that. If he stopped here you know something."

Bernie said. "Well you might have a point there. The man didn't use that name but he did tell me the law was after him back up in Webber's Falls. He said he lucked out when another outlaw picked a fight with the law man that was after him. When he said it was a law man I never dreamed it was you ol' buddy."

Hunter asked. "Is that all he said?" Bernie scratched his head and said. "Just about, but he did say where he was headed."

Hunter waited a little while. Donnie was starting to giggle when Hunter said. "Where, damn it, where?"

Bernie looked at him and said "Texarkana."

Well Hunter thought that would be fine. He'd catch him and put in for the reward and stay home a while. "You don't say" Hunter said.

Bernie grinned and said. "I just did say, weren't you listenin'. I swear, I've known you twenty some years and everything's still gotta be an argument." Hunter smiled a rare smile and shook his head.

Hunter asked. "You got a gunsmith in this town?"

Bernie answered. "Sure we do. He's blind in one eye and can't see out of the other but he's a gunsmith alright, says so on the sign. What's broke?"

Hunter showed him the hammer on the Greener and told the story of the stray bullet breakin' it.

Bernie said. "Leave it here I'll fix it while you two get somethin' to eat. The gunsmith would just bring it to me to fix anyhow. By the way aren't you gonna introduce me to the better lookin half of the gang?" He nodded in Donnie's direction.

Hunter said. "Oh, I forgot with all the bickerin', that's Donnie."

Bernie said. "Good to meet you Donnie, you're not too particular about who you travel with are ya?" Donnie said. "Nah, I guess not." and shot a grin back at Bernie.

Hunter said. "Can you really fix that shotgun?"

Bernie looked genuinely offended and said. "I said I could, didn't I? I'm tired and old and ugly but I can fix anything made of iron, brass copper, or steel." Hunter said. "I knew that, I just wanted to piss you off."

They took the rifles from the Indians down to the hardware and let Bernie get to work. He'd sit and jaw with them until next week if they'd stay and jaw.

The hardware dealer was an unhappy old man named Meeks. Meeks offered Hunter ten dollars each for the rifles. Hunter shook his head. They were worn and scratched but the Winchesters were good rifles. The Henrys were serviceable as well. Hunter said he'd take twenty each for the Winchesters and twelve each for the Henrys. Meeks asked. "You want merchandise or cash?" Hunter said. "Cash if you please. We may spend some of it here but we need to start even." Meeks thought a minute and simply said."Deal", He reached under the counter for the cash box and counted out one hundred and eight dollars. Hunter split it fifty four dollars each and handed Donnie his half. Donnie said. "Mr. Meeks, you got any spurs"? Meeks pointed to the far wall. Donnie found the pair he wanted. He paid the man back seven of his fifty four dollars and went outside to sit on the step and put on his spurs.

They walked back down to the livery. They stopped at the general store hunter bought coffee. Donnie bought two more cans of peaches. The walked back into BF Livery and Blacksmith after about an hour had passed. Bernie was just screwin' the new hammer onto the Greener. He'd cut it out of a horseshoe. He'd done some heatin' and hammerin' and a whole lot of file work. The new hammer looked exactly like its right hand counterpart except it still had a nail hole in the center of it just below the curve. Bernie told him it gave it character. Hunter was inclined to agree.

Bernie asked, "Where'd ya sell them rifles? Hunter told him at the hardware. Bernie said. "You sold 'em to ol' Meeks? I hate that ol' bastard. I wouldn't piss in his ass if his guts were on fire." Donnie broke into a full belly laugh at that. Hunter asked Bernie what they owed, he said. "Four bits for the grain oughta cover it."

Hunter tossed him a dollar. He said. "See you next trip you old bastard."

Bernie said. "That'll work you son-of-a-whore." As they rode off Hunter waved. He genuinely liked Bernie. He was one of the three people hunter considered friends. He guesses four since Donnie came along.

Chapter 14 – Back to Broken Bow··· Broken

That night they camped about 15 miles South of Broken Bow. The found a little clearing and sure enough they found Lowe's old fire spot. They built theirs and cooked squirrel. Hunter told Donnie when they got into Texarkana Marla would make them a pot roast that would melt in their mouth and rabbit and squirrel would be a thing of the past.

He told Donnie that if he wanted to get a job at a ranch

around there he knew people who would put him to work. He told him, "You don't have to decide now, it's just livin' out of a saddlebag, eatin' once a day ain't for everybody. Just give it some thought."

They had been asleep a while, that time when you really get down deep. Usually Hunter would have heard something when he felt a warm wet nudge on his cheek. He opened his eyes and jumped about two feet high. A black bear cub was trying to get into his saddlebag, and Hunter scared him as much as he was scared himself.

Donnie was awake and on the cub as fast as a mountain cat. He was pettin' his head and scratchin' his belly. The cub was bawlin' to beat the band. Hunter said. "Donnie put him down now!" Donnie set the cub down on the edge of the clearing, but it was too late. Hunter heard the branches breaking but the sounds echoed off the close hills. He couldn't quite tell where it was coming from. He drew his Colt from the belt by his saddle and said, "Get ready!" The mama bear burst into the clearing about 6 feet to the left of where Hunter was looking and lunged. Hunter fanned the hammer twice and she died in the air. Her right front paw caught hunter on the left thigh up high and put four deep gashes about eight inches long diagonally across Hunters upper leg. The blood flowed out like a red waterfall. The bear fell in a heap. Donnie was quick again getting Hunter to lie down and getting pressure on the wounds. As soon as the bleeding slowed Donnie started saddling horses. He had to get Hunter back to Broken Bow. He didn't know if there was a doctor there but if there were that many folks in one place someone would know how to stitch this up. He got hunter in the saddle and tied his hands to the saddle horn. He'd lost a lot of blood and was fading in and out. He kept thinking she didn't get the big artery in his leg, or the bleeding wouldn't have stopped till Hunter was dead. Back north they headed in the bright summer moonlight.

Donnie stopped about two miles up the trail to check the wound. Seeping but not too bad. He started to mount up again when he saw him. The cub was sitting in the road about a hundred yards back. Donnie had to think about Hunter if he got him back to Broken Bow in time he would come back tomorrow for the cub.

He stopped twice more in the next 5 hours while riding back through the woods at night to check on Hunter. Once Hunter was awake, and talkin' about the bear.

"I knew she'd come angry when that cub let out that bawl."

Next stop the rope on the horn was holdin' him on. He was slumped over forward asleep or unconscious. Donnie checked his knots and pushed the stirrups up on Hunters boots and away they went again.

Donnie pulled them up in front of BF Livery and Blacksmith just as the sun came up. He beat on the door and Bernie answered it quick; he was dressed and Donnie could smell coffee. Bernie yelled, "What the hell's all the racket." Then he saw Hunter hunched over the saddle. He said, "What the hell happened boy?"

Donnie said, "Bear got him on the thigh. He bled a lot but I got it slowed down and headed back here. Is there someone here a doc or a nurse to sew him up?"

Bernie said, "Aw hell I'll sew him up." I'm tired and old and ugly but I can fix anything." He grinned at Donnie and said. "I'll get Mrs. Coon, she's and old army nurse and the closest thing to a sawbones we got in these parts. Get him in there on my cot. I'll be right back."

Donnie got Hunter down, and helped him inside and laid him down on the blacksmith's bunk. He was getting his boots off when Bernie came in with the nurse.

She was sixty five if she was a day. Grey hair pulled up tight in a bun. She was still in her nightgown and her bosoms were as big as a man's head. She grabbed the boy by his left arm and gently but firmly moved him aside and got some scissors from her bag and cut the denim jeans away from the wound. She said "Fetch me some water boy."

Donnie went out and found a bucket and pumped it full at the well out back. Bernie brought a clean sheet and was tearin it up into rags when Hunter woke up.

He looked at the nurse and said, "What did you do with ol' Sgt. O'Malley."

She looked shocked for a second and said, "I buried him in the French Quarter ten years ago and came home. I married a widower here and will likely bury him too. How'd you know Patrick?"

"I served with him in the War. I was visiting him in the hospital and I saw him slap your behind. He told me you was goin' back to Nawlins with him."

She smiled, and started to tell Hunter somethin', but he was out again. It was just as well what came next wasn't pretty. It took seventy six stitches to close up Frank hunter's leg. "No artery or tendon damage." Mrs. Coon said, as she picked up her tools. She did ask the boy, "What's his name son".

Donnie told her. "Frank Hunter."

She smiled and said Patrick had spoken of him often. She was glad she could help him. She said. "You make him eat. He needs to make some blood to replace what he's lost. I'll come check on him this evenin'." She left Donnie and Bernie sitting in the livery stunned.

Bernie said. "I was gonna have some coffee when you rode up. It's still warm if you want some." Donnie did but what he wanted worse was a little sleep. He went out and unsaddled the horses. He washed the blood off Hunters saddle. He stowed them in the barn and brought his bedroll in with both their saddlebags and Hunters gun belt. He got out a can of peaches and set them by the bed and went to get a cup of Bernie's coffee.

When he got back Hunter was awake. He said, "You damned kid, you saved my life again. I guess I'm gonna have to keep you around."

Donnie said, "Mrs. Coon said to make you eat. I got these peaches here if you want em." Hunter allowed that peaches sounded pretty good right now. Donnie opened the can and handed them over. Hunter didn't think he was really that hungry until he started eating them. He finished the can off in about three minutes. Donnie asked him if he wanted any more.

He said, "In a while maybe, ask ol' Bernie if I can have some of that coffee I smell."

Bernie came in with a cup and a chunk of ham. Hunter drank the coffee and ate the ham. He then told Bernie the story of the bear cub and the momma.

When his part ended Donnie picked up the story and told of how he got Hunter back to town. Then he said, "Oh shit I forgot. I gotta go get that cub. He started saddling his horse."

Hunter said. "You'll never find him now boy."

Donnie said. "I gotta go look."

Hunter was wrong. Donnie found the cub about a mile out of town in a plumb thicket. He gathered him up and took him back to town.

When Donnie pulled up at the livery with the cub across the saddle he looked like he was almost asleep. He dismounted and got the cub down and took him inside. Hunter was sittin' up talking to Bernie between the chores he had. His shredded jeans were hangin down off the edge of the bed. He looked at the cub and shook his head he said. "Goddamn cub... sorry about your momma. She would' a killed me if I hadn't done it."

Bernie walked in and said. "Well there lil' bear, see what you caused?" He stooped down and the cub walked over to him. Bernie scratched his head. He looked at Donnie and said. "I may know what to do with this lil' guy."

Donnie looked at him and said. "They ain't gonna hurt him are they? We already killed his momma."

Bernie said. "If they take him they won't hurt him. They're already raisin a pair of fawns and a baby horned owl that I know of. They feed the fawns goats milk and I bet a bear cub could get by on goats milk too. We'll go talk to em after you tie that cub up in a stall and get some sleep, you look pert' near dead boy."

Donnie was done in, he tied the cub up to a beam in a stall. He protested so Donnie rolled his bedroll out in the stall and laid down there. Him and the cub slept eight hours. It was the cub that woke Donnie up. He was startin' to get hungry. It had been almost a whole day since he had eaten.

Bernie said, "Get saddled and we'll take him out to the Johansen's."

When Donnie got saddled he brought Hunter the other can of peaches and started to open them.

Hunter said, "I can open the damned things boy."

He smiled and Donnie thought he liked Hunters smile; he didn't do it very often, but when he did you knew he meant it. He went to load up the cub. Bernie was waitin' outside and off they went. East of town about two miles was an old farm house with a big barn and chicken coup out back. Bernie had told him on their way out that the Johansen's were a Swedish couple that moved out here a few years back, and that Mrs. Johansen couldn't have babies so she nursed any baby animal she could find.

She met them in the yard. She was a striking blonde woman a full six feet tall. She was beautiful and Donnie was a little taken aback.

Bernie said, "Evenin' Goldie, this is Donnie Hunter, he's a friend of mine who has a problem I think you can fix. Her eyes opened wide when she saw the cub.

She rushed to Donnie's horse and said, "My name is not Goldie. Bernie just calls me that because of my hair. My name is Hilmar Johansen. I am pleased to meet you Mr. Hunter."

Donnie stammered. "Ju just Donnie ma'am. This cub's momma attacked us and we had to shoot her. I just couldn't leave him out there in the woods to die."

Hilmar looked at Donnie and said, "You have brought him to the right place Donnie, I love babies of all kinds. This will be my first bear cub. I'm sure he will drink goat's milk. Why don't we find out?" She cradled the cub in her arms like a human baby and headed out toward the barn. Donnie and Bernie followed her around back.

Bernie asked her, "Goldie, where's Elof today?"

She turned around and said. "Bernie, that's the first time you haven't called him Elf since I've known you. Have you known his name all along?"

Bernie smiled and said, "Goldie, I don't call anyone by their real name. I'm tired, and old, and ugly, I gotta have my fun where I can these days girl."

Hilmar said. "Fun? I just thought you were stupid." She shot Donnie a wink and away she went again. Inside the barn was a cream can full of fresh goat's milk she shook it a little and poured a quart into a bottle used to feed calves and held the nipple out to the cub. First he sniffed then he licked it a little as the milk dripped out his eyes widened a little and he latched onto the nipple. He drained the bottle in a couple of minutes.

Bernie was looking at a big old Morgan gelding in a stall when Hilmar took Donnie's hands in hers and said, "Thank you for bringing him to me Donnie Hunter, I'll keep him till he can go back to the woods. He'll be a great source of joy for me. Do not worry about him. Elof will be home soon. Will you and Bernie stay for supper."

Donnie said, "We can't Ma'am I have to get supper for a friend who was hurt by this cub's momma."

She nodded and said, "Well I can't talk too long, I have a lot to do tonight to get him situated so you gentlemen will have to let me get to work now."

As they walked back up to the road Bernie looked back and said, "Goldie, you tell ol' Elf to bring that Morgan into the shop next week. He's got a loose shoe that needs attention. I may be tired, and old, and ugly, and stupid, but I can fix a loose shoe."

Hilmar walked up and leaned down and kissed Bernie's cheek and said, "You're not stupid, Bernie. Thank you for bringing him to me. I'll tell Elof about the shoe. Now you go and let me get busy."

They rode back to town while Bernie told Donnie if he was 20 years younger and a little taller he would shoot ol' Elf Johansen in the head and come a courtin' Goldie hisself. She was a fine figure of a woman and strong. He bet she could wrestle that bear cub's momma and fare better than ol' Frank Hunter.

When they got back to town Bernie boiled potatoes while Donnie tended the horses.

Hunter was still in the bed when Mrs. Coon walked in. She went straight to Hunter and said, "Mr. Hunter, I have something of Patrick's I want you to have. He told me you were the bravest man he'd ever met. He bought these from a river boat gambler who needed a stake. He was going to give them to you when you came to Nawlins to visit. I've kept them these years as a memento. I never expected to meet you, but I'm glad I did. They might save your life someday." She handed him a wood box.

He opened it and revealed a fine pair of nickel plated Remington Derringers. The caliber was .41 rimfire and there were 50 rounds in the box.

Hunter said. "I can't take these, they're yours".

She shook her head and said, "They were yours the minute Patrick bought them from that gambler. He never even fired them once. He cleaned and oiled them every now and then. He bought that box of cartridges and put it in there and kept them for you. He always said "If I die before Frank Hunter comes down, you give him this box, woman." She smiled at that. Some men have sweet names for their wives, Honey, Sweetie, Sugar Pie. Woman was what Patrick O'Malley had called her and she loved the sound of it. She had loved that old war horse and now after he had been gone ten years she was still doin' his bidding. She continued, "You're gonna take those pistols, Mr. Hunter, or I'm gonna give em' to old Bernie here and he ain't deservin' of anything 'cept a boot in the ass.

Bernie smiled and said, "Well I love you too Mrs. Coon."

Hunter said, "We can't let that happen. I'll take em' and thank you, Mrs. Coon, for carryin' them around all these years.

I'll put em to work."

She said. "Now let's have a look at that leg." She unwrapped it and cleaned it off. It was already scabbing over. She said. "You gotta keep this clean or it will infect Mr. Hunter. A little rubbing alcohol on a cloth around the wounds, keep the wounds dry and clean for two weeks. Then the stitches can come out. Will you be stayin' here for the two weeks?"

Hunter replied. "I'll prob'ly be leavin' soon as I can ride Ma'am".

She said. "Better wait a couple of days before you do. Is there someone who can take out the stitches for you where you are going?"

Hunter thought of the times Marla had nursed him and nodded with a smile. "Yes Ma'am there is. She'll do it for me again I expect."

Mrs. Coon said. "Good, I'll be back in a couple of days to check it before you leave. Keep eatin and be careful when you walk. Don't mess up my beautiful needle-work. I'd better get home now, good night gentlemen, you too Bernie'." She threw him a wink. Hunter thought Bernie'd be the next husband she buried if he wasn't careful and smiled a bit to himself.

Chapter 15 – Goin' Home

Hunter spent the next two days movin' slow around the livery. The pain wasn't as bad as the itch, it was maddening. Donnie got four more cans of peaches. He ate one himself, Hunter ate the others. He remarked on how he was gonna have to get another saddlebag now just to carry damned peaches.

The second evening Mrs. Coon came by to check his leg and tell them goodbye. Hunter thanked her and asked her what he owed. She said, "If you got it I could use a few dollars for silk thread you used all my stock with yer big old gashes."

Hunter reached into his hat and came out with five twenty dollar gold pieces and put them on the table by the bed. He said,

"OK Mrs. Coon here's three dollars for thread, ninety seven dollars for savin' my life."

She said, "The boy saved your life. I just did the sewing."

Hunter said, "I know that, but we're partners. That's his job; just like it's my job to help him now. We share everything and we are responsible for each other. It goes with the job. I never thought I'd be around people enough to share a meal let alone have a partner on the trail. The boy needed me when I found him and I could see somethin' in him. As it turns out I needed him too, he's saved my life twice now. I hope to return the favor if he gets in a fix."

She said, "Frank, that boy worships you. You think about the things you teach him and the way you treat other people. He's gonna be your carbon copy someday. Patrick told me you were the best he'd ever seen with a gun. You had no pause killin' someone who needed killin'. Patrick was the same way. Teach Donnie well, like Patrick taught you."

Hunter assured her he would and she headed home stopping on her way out to pester Ol' Bernie.

Hunter called Donnie in and opened the wood box. He gave Donnie one of the Derringers and opened the box of shells.

Donnie said. "These were a gift to you, I can't take this".

"Nonsense," Hunter said, "In a box they are nothing but dead weight to carry. If we put em to work they earn their keep. O'Malley would have wanted us to use em' that's why he bought em'. I don't need two. Load it and put it in your right front pocket. Get used to puttin' all you other stuff in your left pocket. Always have this in your right. Don't ever pull it out until the man you need to shoot is within ten feet. I've seen a .41 rimfire bounce off a coyotes head at twenty feet. Aim for somethin' soft."

Donnie took the pistol and loaded it and put it in his pocket and put the other shells in his saddlebag.

Bernie had been stewin' the end of that ham with some brown beans all afternoon, and they were smellin' pretty good.

He poked his head in and told them the cornbread was almost done. They needed to come fix a plate. They did what they were told. The beans tasted better than they smelled. All three of them laughed at Bernie's stories and feasted. In the morning Hunter and Donnie would head to Hunters farm house in Texarkana. They were still a long way from home.

Donnie was up before the sun fixin' coffee. Hunter woke up and winced at the pain but it was just pulling at the stitches. He could feel it healing. He had the alcohol in the bag to keep it clean till Marla could work on it some more. They were still three or four days away from Texarkana. Hunter would take it easy.

Hunter said, "Bernie what do I owe you for puttin' us up and feedin' us I do appreciate all the help."

He said. "You don't owe me a thing. I'm flush at the moment. Tell you what, come back in the fall and we'll go deer huntin'. I may be tired, and old, and ugly but I can still out hunt a limpin' bounty hunter."

Hunter said, "It's a date Bernie, It's been good to see you again. I do hope I'm gone longer than twelve hours this time".

Bernie said, "Considerin' the last trip, I do too Hunter. You boys be careful out there and come back anytime."

They waved and again they rode south, not as urgent this time. Hunter suspected that Lowe would be waiting in Texarkana....He was.

They passed the dead momma bear around noon. She was gettin' almost as ripe as ol' Big Jim had. They headed on South and camped on a creek bank about half way to the Red River.

Donnie shot two rabbits and spit roasted them for a change. Hunter sat watchin' the fire flare up from the fat that was dripping off the rabbits. They ate and Donnie had a can of peaches while Hunter cleaned his wound with the alcohol.

"Tomorrow we'll cross into Texas" Hunter said, "Once we do we need to be a little more careful. Folks, other than Indians, have been livin' in Texas for a hundred years or more. Here in the Nations, they've stayed out for the most part. That's why the

Gov'ment gave it to the Indians. They took their good land and sent 'em here. It won't last though. I may not live to see it but the gov'ment 'll take this from 'em too. You wait'n see".

Hunter had three sips out of his bottle of bourbon to try and calm the itching and tried to sleep. They were in Choctaw country now. He felt relatively safe here. You still needed to be aware though. Three sips was enough.

They crossed the Red River late in the afternoon the next day. It ran muddy and wide with the spring melt from it's headwater in the New Mexico Mountains. Once in Texas they stopped to dry off from the crossing. Donnie undressed and washed off in the river. Hunter re-cleaned and dried his wounds. He didn't think the muddy water would hurt it but better safe than sorry.

Donnie put on the spare drawers he'd bought in Ft. Smith and left the old ones hangin' on the limb by the river. If someone wanted to wash the smell of his butt out of them they were welcome to them.

Hunter said, "I know how we could have something for supper, besides rabbit if your game."

Donnie allowed how he was getting tired of rabbits too, he was game.

Hunter said, "Get them clothes off, and put your old drawers back on. You're goin' swimmin'."

Donnie did as he was told. They walked along the river bank till they found a place where the running water had found a recess on the bank and was swirling. Hunter said, "Go in the water downstream of that swirl, then feel your way back up the bank for holes in the mud. Real slow stick your hand in the hole and feel for a catfish. If you feel a turtle get you hand out quick or you won't get it all back. Use your left hand. Never noodle with your gun hand."

"Noodle?" Donnie asked.

"Yeah that's what we call it in Texas. In Arkansas they just call it hand fishin', they got no imagination. Once you feel a catfish rub his nose. As muddy as this water is he can't see a thing. He'll open his mouth and try to bite you but he has no teeth, just little bristles. It'll smart some and you'll loose some hide but it's worth it if you're hungry. I'd do it, but I gotta keep my leg dry."

Donnie said, "Lucky you." Then stepped back into the Red River.

Hunter said, "Once your hand is in his mouth grab his bottom jaw and hold on. When you pull him out of the hole, wrap him around your waist with your other hand and carry him out.

Donnie did as he was told. Hunter was proud of him doing this without question. Hunter asked him, and he did it. Blind trust was a good thing as long as you picked the right person to trust.

Donnie was feeling along the bank and found the first hole and plunged his hand in and a twenty pound catfish nearly knocked him down leaving the hole.

"Slowly!" Hunter said, "you gotta sneak up on 'em."

On the next hole Donnie slid his hand in slowly and felt the fish. When he first touched it he started a bit but forced his nerves to be calm enough to do this. He rubbed the catfish on the nose he could feel the slick smooth skin, he felt the whiskers. As he moved down the catfish's face he turned his hand palm down and the catfish opened up his mouth just like Hunter had said he would. Donnie allowed the catfish to mouth his hand till it got worked in. The fish bit down, and it was more than a little painful, but he grabbed the fish's bottom jaw, and pulled him out of the hole. When the fish's tail cleared the edge of the bank he thrashed it around and squarely hit Donnie in the side of the head with it, but Donnie didn't let go. He was busy trying to gather up that tail with his right hand. He finally got ahold of it and pulled it tight to his right side. He had the fish trapped, or the fish had him. He was afraid of what his poor left hand looked like. It felt like a hundred needles were stabbing it. He walked back to where he walked in. Hunter helped him out of the river, and they laid the fish down on the bank and pried the fish's mouth open with a stick. It was a beauty, about fifteen pounds.

Hunter said, "Donnie, I believe that's the biggest channel cat I've ever seen. You did a damned fine job. Let's look at that hand." Donnie was grinning ear to ear he hadn't thought about the hand until Hunter mentioned it. He looked down and the blood was dripping off the end of his fingers. The excitement had cancelled out the pain. He walked to the river and washed it. It wasn't as bad as it looked. Though there were a couple of pretty good size spots where the top layer of hide was gone, it looked more like a burn.

Hunter dug around in his saddle bags and got some of his bandage and the alcohol. Good thing he had this. His little bottle of bourbon was getting low. Hunter dressed and wrapped Donnie's hand then set about building a fire. "Catfish for supper!" Hunter exclaimed. He looked at Donnie who was still smiling and said, "Go shoot us a possum."

"Why do we need a possum?" Donnie asked,

"You can fry rabbit dry, they have some fat in 'em, catfish don't. We'll fry the possum and render the fat then fry the catfish in possum fat."

Donnie went huntin'. He shot a fat possum fifteen minutes later. It looked like a big rat. They are greasy. Preston had fed him possum stew his whole childhood. Donnie didn't care if he never ate another possum.

When Donnie got back to the river Hunter had a fire going and the catfish was cut into six big catfish steaks. They were salted and peppered and waiting on the side of Hunters saddlebags.

"Skin that possum Donnie let's get 'er goin."

Donnie made short work of the possum. It wasn't his first. They fried the possum and he rendered a half inch of fat in the little skillet. Hunter fried the steaks two at a time and laid them back on the saddle bag. Donnie ate the first two while they were still hot enough to burn his tongue. They were delicious. Hunter ate three of the last four and Donnie only ate the last one when Hunter assured him he was as full as a tick.

They slept on the bank of the Red River that night, one with a throbbing leg, one with a shredded hand and were content and happy. Hunter thought, "Funny what a little change of diet can do.

Chapter 16 – Texarkana

The next evening they reigned up in front of a little white frame house about a mile West of Texarkana, Texas. The place was freshly painted the windows were clean. They led their horses to the corral. Unsaddled them, Then poured both their canteens down the well pump to wet the leather down there, and filled the water trough with the well pump.

Hunter told Donnie they'd buy some grain tomorrow. They went in the house with a key that was hanging on a nail in the barn. The wood box was full, the pantry was stocked with mason jars of fruit, beans, and vegetables. There was some canned meat in there as well.

Hunter said, "Eat what you want, I'll be back." He walked across the yard to his Momma's marker. Whoever painted the house this time had painted the marker as well.

It still looked like it did those nineteen years ago. Augustine Hunter – Died Sick. Not much to say about his mother's life he thought. He thought about all the outlaws he'd tracked and taken. What did their markers say? Lazy T – Died Desperate? Or Big Jim Barrington – Died Surprised? Frank thought mostly they all died scared. That was a shame but it was the life they chose.

When Hunter came back in Donnie had a fire in the stove and had a pretty good smelling soup goin with some canned vegetables and some canned meat.

"Smells good Kid." He sat down in a chair for the first time since he was at BF Livery and Blacksmith. He dropped the pants he'd bought in Broken Bow, and cleaned his wounds. They were healing nicely. The itching wasn't as bad today.

He laid out his tools, to clean them. The sheriff's model that had been in the saddle bag since the weather warmed up got the full treatment first.

Hunter went to a cupboard in the small living room and brought out a box with his cleaning supplies and tools for gunsmithing. On top was a towel that was oil soaked and greasy. He laid the towel out on the table and went to work. He began completely disassembling the guns, cleaning, oiling, and wiping them dry with an old torn cotton shirt. Last was the new Derringer the old nurse had given him. It hadn't been out of his pocket since he put it there. It was really dirty. It looked new when Hunter was done.

Donnie watched the cleaning while Hunter worked. Hunter told him things to do when he cleaned his after supper. "Don't let this spring get away, and the carrier block on your rifle needs to be cleaned and dry. Too much oil collects dirt there." Donnie watched all this with the interest of a disciple listening to a prophet.

After the soup, which was very good, Donnie cleaned his guns. The Remington broke down a little different than Hunter's Colts but the idea was the same. His guns cleaned Donnie asked where Hunter wanted him to bunk.

Hunter pointed at two doors on the east end of the house. "Pick one, two rooms, two beds both the same."

Donnie picked up his saddle bags and went to bed. Hunter finished off the bourbon and turned in himself.

The next morning broke hot and sultry the way a summer day always does along the Texas-Louisiana line. The locusts were whirring by 8:00 am, and it was ninety degrees in the shade. Hunter and Donnie saddled up and headed to town.

"Breakfast in a café." That's what they were after, then to the feed and grain store, then to the Three Doors for a cool beer. Cool was as cool as it would get in the old cellar under the tongue and groove floor.

They got their breakfast at a place called Mamma Carol's Kitchen. "This is new." Hunter said as they tied up out front. Hunter told Donnie, "Last time I was home this was a dry goods store.' They went inside and sat at a long counter on stools with shiny nickel plated legs. The wood burning stove was behind the counter with a pot of coffee steaming on the back burner. Hunter told the lady behind the counter. "We'll both have a cup of that coffee, if it's fresh." The lady behind the counter was in her forties she was round in all the right places. She was pleasant to look at, cheerful to talk to, and her auburn hair was graying at the temples

"Just made it, Mister. It's as fresh as it can be and not be a bean." The coffee was as good as advertised. There were hand-written menus on the counter. Hunter had biscuits and gravy while Donnie had ham and eggs. Both of them had a pile of home fried potatoes. Donnie still marveled that someone would cook you a meal, and then bring it to you, and you didn't even have to wash a dish.Donnie settled up with Mama Carol after a third cup of that coffee.

After they ate they went to the feed store and bought three fifty pound sacks of rolled oats. The man at the feed store remembered Hunter alright. He allowed he had three other deliveries out that way this afternoon, and he'd glad to drop this off too. The bill came to three dollars even. Hunter paid the bill, since Donnie had picked up the breakfast check. They rode out to the north end of the main street and reigned up in front of the Three Doors Saloon.

The saloon was a big old clapboard, two story structure with a covered boardwalk that went all the way around three sides. Balconies from the upstairs rooms were above the boardwalk. A few girls that worked in the saloon were having coffee on the balcony displaying their wares to the passers by.

The men folk didn't seem to mind a bit.

The church goin' Baptist ladies of Texarkana seemed to take a dimmer view of a buxom twenty-two year old havin' coffee on the balcony in her petticoat and bustle.

Frank thought it was a welcome sight, "Home again," he muttered. Donnie just gawked and blushed.

Inside the saloon there were few customers this early in the day, but there was a poker game goin' on that looked like it'd been going all night. Hunter bellied up to the bar. A big, blonde, balding man came from the back room and said what'll it be stranger then the recognition showed on his face. "Hunter!" he exclaimed.

"Good to see you, Steve." Frank said.

"How long's it been Frank?"

Hunter scowled, "six months."

Sanders went on, "Well at least you're home for the hot part of the summer."

"I ain't home, Steve, the trail just led me through here. By the way," Hunter took the poster on Lowe out of his shirt pocket. "You seen this guy around here?"

Steve Sanders took the poster from Hunter and looked at it in disbelief. This guys been here for a while Frank. He seems like an OK guy. Plays some cards, drinks beer, and waits. He's always sittin in the back corner watchin' the doors.

"He's watchin for me," Hunter said as he took the poster and folded it. I had him in Webber's Falls but was unavoidably detained. When was he here last?

Steve said, "Last Night, he comes in most every night. I think he's rented a house over on the north side of town".

Hunter thought if he rented a house he'll stay a month anyway.

Hunter said, "Steve give us two piss-warm beers here if you please.

Steve asked, "Is this the famous Donnie Hunter we've all heard s'much about?"

Hunter allowed that it was with a nod. He took off his hat and dropped it on a table and asked "Where is she Steve?"

Donnie sat down and sipped his piss-warm beer.

Steve said, "She's out of town on an errand, the nature of said errand she would not divulge to me. She did say if you came home not to let you leave till she got back."

Hunter asked when she left.

Steve said she'd been gone a week, and she had told him she'd be back in ten days when she left.

Sanders walked around the bar and sat down at the table and looked Donnie up and down. He said, "You're a fine strappin' young man. What are ya doin' trailin' around the Indian Nation with a ruffian like Frank Hunter? He'll lead you to no good."

"He saved my life,Mister," Donnie said over his mug.

"Well the debt's been repaid Donnie. You give some thought to what I told you, not everyone's built to live out of a saddlebag."

They had one more beer and set out for the house. Hunter was lost in his thoughts while they rode the few miles out to the Hunter farm as the town-folk called the place, although it hadn't been farmed in twenty years or more.

When they had the horses put away, and a generous dose of oats set out for 'em Donnie asked, "We gonna go take him tonight?"

Hunter's brow furrowed and he said, "I don't think so, and I'll tell you why. Marla NEVER leaves town. As far as I know this is the only time she's been more than ten miles away from The Three Doors in the 20 years I've known her. Women of her profession usually move around following the silver strikes or the cattle herds. Workin' men with big pay to spend. She's been happy to stay here and work this saloon. Sometimes the money's bigger than others sometimes it's not, but she's rooted here. Something important got her to leave even if only for ten days. Lowe's rented a house. His rent's payed up for two more weeks anyway. We'll wait a few days and see if Marla's OK. I just won't go in The Three Doors till then. You on the other hand, will become a regular."

Lowe had not seen Donnie at Webber's Falls. Donnie had poked the shotgun through the batwing doors and fired. Lowe was out the window and gone before the doors had opened.

Just before dark that night they rode back into town. Donnie had studied the picture on the poster for an hour. He had memorized every curve, and wrinkle on the mans face.

When they reached the street the saloon was on Hunter reined the big gelding up and said "I'll wait here. You leave that pistol in your saddlebag. Like I told you, never wear it in a saloon unless you're takin' a bounty. Some drunk could call you out for no reason and you'd have to kill him just because he had three too many shots of the mule piss Sanders passes off as rye whiskey. Keep the derringer in you pocket."

Donnie unbuckled his gun belt and stowed it in his saddlebag. He nodded at Hunter and rode the last two blocks alone.

17 – Watchin for Days

Donnie walked into The Three Doors Saloon and looked around at the walls. The place was a lot more impressive at night with all the lamps lit. It seemed brighter in here tonight than it did this afternoon. Three poker games were goin' on and the girls from the balcony were moving among the patrons serving drinks, sitting on laps. Occasionally one would head upstairs with one of the cowboys.

Hunter had told him back at the house "Don't let them girls know what's under your hat or they'll tear a young kid like you apart. They look sweet, but when it comes to money a whore is meaner than that momma bear."

Donnie stood at the bar and got another piss-warm beer. He sipped it. He'd seen Lowe when he walked in but didn't stare. He watched the girls a while and listened to the chips on the tables click against each other when the gamblers called or raised. He took it all in and watched David Lowe in the corner. He sat there backed into the corner. The spacing of the table was different than the others Donnie could tell it had been moved. Lowe wanted an unobstructed view of all three doors, and he watched them like a hawk. The girls didn't bother with him he had apparently warned them off earlier.

It was at this time when one of them walked up to Donnie. She asked "What's a sweet kid like you doin' drinkin' beer in here? How old are you kid?"

Donnie said, "I was thirsty and old enough ma'am."

"Ma'am!" she exclaimed. "Ain't you a fine young gentleman. Why were you thirsty? Mommy's tit go dry? You can try one of mine if you have two dollars." She brushed her breasts against Donnie's strong right arm.

He remembered what Hunter had said and told her "I just have fifty cents left and I'm still kinda thirsty."

She looked him in the eye and said, "Well kid if you come up with two dollars you come back and ask for Rhonda. I'll take care of you like your mommy never did. You hear me kid?"

Donnie nodded and said, "Yes Ma'am I hear you."

She meandered away looking for the cowboy with two dollars. Donnie thought to himself that after they collected the bounty on Lowe that Rhonda was gonna get two dollars several times.

Lowe sat there sipped beer and spoke to no one that night. He didn't play cards. He didn't go upstairs, and at around ten o'clock he got up and walked out.

Hunter had noticed a gap between the hardware store and the barber shop just big enough to back a horse into. He backed the gelding in there far enough he was in complete darkness. Hell, Hunter was four feet away, and he couldn't see him. He walked back to the street end of the gap and tried not to scratch the stitches in his leg. He watched the saloon.

He watched a few patrons come and go. He wondered if Donnie was upstairs yet. Hell he would've been if he was in Donnie's shoes. He had a feeling though that Donnie would wait till the job was done. His commitment was strong. About an hour and a half went by, and Lowe came out and mounted the same horse he'd fled Webber's Falls on. The same horse ol' Bernie had shod for him.

He walked the horse up the street past Hunter in his hiding place. Hunter prayed his gelding didn't whinny a greeting to Lowe's horse. He didn't this time. Hunter would leave the horse somewhere else tomorrow. That was careless. He hadn't thought that Lowe would ride right past him. About ten minutes later Donnie came out and rode up the street. Hunter rode out of the gap in the buildings. They went home.

About half way back to the house Donnie said, "Tomorrow we need to go in a little earlier and I need to take two more dollars." Hunter smiled in the dark and just said OK.

All the next day Hunter sat thinking trying to figure out what Marla was doing and where she'd gone. For the life of him he couldn't think of why she'd left Texarkana. If something was wrong with Becca she would have gotten word to him. If she was in trouble she knew he was going to take care of it.

They had supper and headed into town about an hour earlier tonight than last night. They separated at the same place as last night. There was a billiard parlor about a block up the street so Hunter rode up there and tied his horse at the rail and walked back to the gap in the buildings. There was a wooden box on the boardwalk in front of the hardware store, hunter grabbed it for a stool. He sat down with his back against the hardware store side wall deep in the gap and waited.

Donnie walked into the saloon just as he had the night before. There was a card game going on at Lowe's table but Lowe himself was seated in the same chair still had a clear view of all three doors. He played card looking at, and over his hand when he played. He watched the doors when he folded. Donnie went to the bar and got a beer. It was a little cooler than last nights but not much.

He'd been there a bit when Rhonda walked over and said,

"My young gentleman is back again. Did you bring your two dollars tonight love?"

Donnie said "As a matter of fact I did Ma'am. I'm an orphan and my momma never took care of me at all so I guess I'll have to rely on you."

Rhonda told him that two dollars would get him a half hour of care, and seeing how young he was, she allowed he could probably get cared for three times in a half hour. She was right on the money.

He came downstairs and the poker game was starting to thin out. There were still four players, but two of them were low on chips and Lowe was one of them. Donnie thought it would be hard to watch your cards, the other players, and the three doors at the same time. It was then he realized he was grinning like an idiot.

He was grinning and couldn't stop. He concentrated hard on keeping a straight face and finally succeeded. He looked up and realized how they would take Lowe. The stairs led up the side of the saloon to the girl's rooms upstairs. There was a balcony that ran around three sides inside just like outside. If they went up the side of the building they could get in through one of those rooms and into the saloon without going through any of those three doors. The stairs came down into the saloon behind Lowe's table.

Hunter left his hiding spot and walked up the street away from The Three Doors. Lowe had ridden up the street into the darkness last night. Hunter wanted to see where he lived. He walked up into the darkness. The lamps ended about a block from hunters hiding spot but the town went on for five more blocks. Hunter walked three blocks into the dark. He found a bush that looked like good cover and sat down behind it. He listened to the crickets, and watched the moon, and wondered where the hell Marla was.

Lowe got up from the game when he'd lost his last hand. He tipped a wave at Steve and shuffled out the batwings to the street. Donnie sat there grinning for ten more minutes.

Steve asked him if he wanted another beer or a rag to wipe that stupid grin off his face.

Donnie told him he had to go.

Steve knew Hunter was waitin' outside for him. Steve asked Donnie if Hunter was waitin' for Marla to get back before he took Lowe.

Donnie looked at Sanders and said you'll have to ask Hunter that. He finished the last of his beer and headed outside.

Out at the hitchin' rail he was getting on his horse when he heard a voice from above say "Bring your two dollars again tomorrow young gentleman. I'd love to take care of you some more.

He tipped his Stetson and said, "I may do it Ma'am, I may do it." He rode up the street… Grinning like an idiot.

Hunter sat in the bushes thinking and listening to crickets when he saw Lowe coming up the street. His gelding was at a slow walk. He was lit up well till he passed the billiard hall. He looked in through the glass, and Hunter thought he was going to stop but he kept coming.

He rode past Hunter a half block and pulled into a little yellow frame house. He got down and led the horse around back into a little corral in the back with a shed and a lean to. Hunter could see he was un-saddling the horse, so he headed back down the street to the pool hall to get his horse. He mounted up about the time Donnie was coming into view. He could see the grin from a block away.

They rode in silence until Hunter said, "I can hear that smile from here."

Donnie said, "I can't stop I'm sorry."

Hunter said, "No need to be sorry… Smile away partner. Rhonda likes the young ones. I think she likes to break 'em in her way."

Donnie said, "How'd you know it was Rhonda?"

Hunter said, "She always gets the young ones. Prob'ly said

you were a good gentleman then rubbed her boobs on you. She has a routine. It works, and from the grins I've seen coming down the stairs it's worth the two dollars."

Donnie allowed it surely was.

On their way back to the farm Donnie told Hunter about Lowe's losing at cards and how he watched those doors all the time. He told him he had an idea. Hunter said, "Come in over the balcony and come down the stairs behind him?"

"Yes" Donnie said disappointed.

Hunter said "Great minds think alike Donnie. I thought of it sittin' in the bushes up the street tonight."

Donnie told Hunter that Sanders asked when you were gonna take him.

Hunter cocked his head and said, "He did did he? What did you tell him?"

Donnie said, "I told him he'd have to ask you that. I was just here for a beer.

Hunter told him that was the perfect answer. "Always remember, your business is almost always none of their business. If a man with paper on him is living in a town and the Sheriff or town Marshall finds out he'll catch him for the reward. The US marshals will usually not cut you out. If anyone, like Steve knows your plans they can try to cut you out. Keep 'em in the dark and guessin'. It's always worked for me."

They went home and went to bed; Hunter thinking and Donnie grinning.

18 – Marla's Home

They watched David Lowe for two more nights. His pattern didn't change. Donnie spent two more dollars on Rhonda. She was good for Donnie she built his confidence. The next morning

Hunter and Donnie went to town for breakfast. Hunter knew this was the tenth day.

As they were eating, an old covered wagon came rolling into town from the south. It was chock full of furniture and trunks and crates. It didn't stop though, they just turned the corner, and headed west. Hunter thought it odd that they didn't stop for supplies or water or anything. He just kept watching and eating his breakfast. They hung around town till noon with no sign of Marla. They headed back to the farm, riding along the road on top of the tracks left by that old covered wagon.

They turned into the farm to find that old wagon stopped in front of Hunter's barn. Two women were taking the furniture from the wagon and carrying it into the barn. They pulled up and got down just as Marla came out of the barn. She ran and kissed Hunter deeply then held him tight. You could tell she missed him a lot when he was gone. She was a beautiful woman in her early forties. The soft smooth skin on her face showed she'd never worked a day in the sun. She had a big bonnet on now to keep the sun off her face.

She said, "I've missed you Frank."

Hunter said, "Marla this is…"

She cut him off, "Donnie Hunter?" She stuck out her hand, "I am glad to make your acquaintance."

Donnie shook her hand which was as soft as her face looked.

She elbowed Frank and said, "Rhonda's gonna love this one." Donnie Blushed bright red.

Marla looked at Frank. Frank simply said, "Twice so far."

She looked at Frank for a minute, drinking him in with her eyes. Then she said, "I have someone to introduce to you, Frank, come in the barn." They walked in and a handsome brunette woman. Tall with a good strong backbone stood up from the crate she was looking into. Marla said, "Frank I'd like you to meet Texarkana's new school teacher, Elizabeth Lewis… Liz Hunter Lewis."

Understanding dawned in Hunter's face like a Mountain

sunrise. This was his sister, whom he had loved, and couldn't find after the war. He hugged her. She looked uncomfortable, after all, she was eight years old the last time she'd seen him. This was the closest Frank had been to tears since he found his Momma's grave.

They walked to the house and sat down and Marla told the story. Liz had been taken to Dallas by Momma's cousin when Momma took ill. Typhoid it had been. They raised her, and sent her to school. She had married another school teacher in Dallas, Richard Lewis.

Hunter thought to himself, "Must not be kin to Ol' Lazy T."

Marla said, "It happened that Richard had been killed in an accident in Dallas on a summer job last summer, and Liz had sent a telegram to Texarkana looking for you Frank. The Sheriff brought the telegram to me and I wrote back to Liz. We've been writing back and forth for five months now. She's got the job of school teacher here and we were putting her things in the barn. I thought you wouldn't mind if she stayed here till she gets settled."

Hunter was stunned. He'd believed she was dead for all those years. He didn't even know Momma *had* a cousin in Dallas. Still here she was. She still looked the same as she did when he left home with a bag of bread and cheese all those years ago.

Frank said, "Liz, this house is yours if you want it. You have just as much right to it as I do prob'ly more. I left after Pop. You had to stay and watch Momma get sick and die. I'll get my stuff out tonight if you want it."

Liz said, "Frank I don't want this house. To some folks a house is just sticks and nails put together to keep the rain out. To me this old house has too many memories. There would be a ghost sittin' in every corner. I just need a place till I'm settled. I sold our... my house in Dallas. I have enough to get started here. Back home where I have family. Richard and I never had children so. Big Brother, your all I have left.'

Hunter asked her, "Did Marla tell you what I do for a

living?"

She nodded.

He told her, "It's all I know how to do. I'm gone for weeks sometimes months at a time."

She said, "that's OK, Frank, I'll still have the brother that saved us; Me and Momma from that monster." She told Frank that she'd just stay here till she found a place in town. This was too far to ride to school everyday especially when it rained. Marla had offered to stay out here with her. Frank allowed that him and Donnie would sleep in the barn for a while. It was still better than the trail they'd been on for weeks. Liz said tomorrow she'd go to town and look for a place. Hunter said he knew a little yellow frame house that was coming up for rent soon.

While Hunter and Liz were talking in the kitchen, Donnie had been putting away the horses along with the team from the wagon. He had them hayed and watered and sat down in the shade on the north side of the barn. He was thinking about David Lowe, and how he needed to practice his shooting some; he hadn't practiced since they got into Texarkana. That was when Marla came around the corner. She was breathtakingly beautiful. Donnie was trying not to stare as she sat down next to him.

She said, "Well young man, what's your story."

Donnie looked up at this beautiful woman and opened his mouth to say he didn't have a story, but her kind eyes wouldn't let him lie, so he began.

19 – One Big Happy Family

Donnie told Marla about Preston, and how Preston had traded his folks for him. He told her of the night he hit Preston with a shovel and saved the little Indian girl. He told of the days he ran from him in The Territories. He told her of how Hunter had almost shot him in the sod house and how he'd treated him with kindness for the first time in his life. Marla could see the similarities in their lives. She knew all about Frank's Pop and what he was like. She was starting to understand why Frank had befriended this boy.

She eyed Donnie and said, "How old are you Donnie?"

He answered, "Sixteen, Ma'am, I think."

Donnie went on to tell her of how Preston had caught up with them on the trail. How he'd hired trackers to find him. He told her of how they came into the camp with their guns drawn.

Marla said, "That was a big mistake. Frank will fight with whatever you bring to a fight. If they'd wanted a fist fight he would have obliged them but if you pull a gun on Frank Hunter you need to have your affairs in order."

Donnie went on about how Hunter had killed them all in a wink on an eye without a miss. Marla allowed that Frank never misses. Then he told her of their trip to Webber's Falls and how ol' Big Jim fell in their laps.

It was about then that Liz came around the corner and told them supper was about done. The three of them walked back to the house together. These two women had one of Donnie's hands in theirs. He'd never been happier.

They went inside to the smell of soup and fresh cornbread.

Frank said, "We'll have to get some chickens so we can have some meat that's not canned." He looked around the table and smiled. He thought to himself, "A whore, a school teacher, an orphan, and a bounty hunter, one big happy family." They ate. Frank knew right then that this wouldn't last. The walls would start closing in on him soon but for now it was alright. Tomorrow evening he would collect David Lowe and turn him in for the reward and stay home till the weather cooled off. Well that was the plan anyway.

The next day was cloudy with those high, hot summer clouds that blow past the sun and make it alternately shady then hot. Donnie and Hunter were stacking Liz's things in the barn. "Damned women don't know how to use the available space." Hunter grumbled. When they started the whole barn floor was covered with boxes and trunks. When they finished there was a neat stack of things in one unused corner. Hunter told Donnie, "You can't get in 'em but we're not trippin over 'em."

Around five in the evening Hunter told Donnie, "Well, let's go get our card player." They saddled up and headed to town at a slow pace. Hunter told Donnie he'd decided not to collect him in the saloon. He'd had a better idea. He told Donnie about the little corral and shed behind Lowe's rented house.

They tied up their horses behind Lowe's house about a hundred yards away. They walked in through the trees. About twenty yards from the back yard Hunter stopped and they hunkered down out of sight. Hunter said, "I'm going to get into that shed. His saddle and tack are in there. He'll head to the Three Doors about seven o'clock. He always rides even though it's only seven blocks. I want you to move off to the left here and get where that shed ain't in your line if fire. Wait there with your rifle. I'll confront him when he comes for his saddle. He'll have two choices either stand and fight there, or flee. I don't think he'll go back to the house because he'd be trapped in there. I think he'll flee into these woods. If he does then he falls to you. If he come this way with a gun in his hand you take him down." Donnie nodded. He was ready. Hunter headed into the shed. What he hadn't counted on was Lowe's third choice.

Shortly, Lowe came out the front door of the house and walked back around the near side. He came into the little corral and stuck out his hand. The horse came to him and ate the three sugar cubes he held there. Lowe took hold of his halter and led him to the shed. When he opened the door Hunter was standing there. Lowe just said, "I've been expecting you. I won't give you a reason to shoot me. I've felt you following me since Poteau. I knew you were coming. I know that kid's been watching me between his trips upstairs with Rhonda. I am tired of running from you. I couldn't believe you followed me to Webber's Falls. What is the reward on me anyway?"

Hunter grunted, "Five Hundred."

"Whew" Lowe hissed. "I guess they're fond of their constables in Decatur, Texas. I didn't want to shoot him but he didn't give me another choice. I just needed a stake and that bank was just sittin' there full of money. It's about all gone now, the money that is. Gambled it away, drank it up, rented this house. I was 'bout to start lookin' for work when that kid showed up in the saloon. He the one who shot Big Jim through the door?" Hunter nodded.

"He saved your ass that day man. What's your name anyway."

"Frank Hunter.

" Lowe smiled at that and just said "Good Fit."

Frank was kinda taken aback by Lowe's demeanor. He was calm, and to be honest he seemed relieved. Frank had never collected a bounty when the guy had wanted to be caught. He only went after the dead or alive outlaws. That always meant they were gonna swing for what they'd done. Murder, horse stealin', and cattle rustlin' were all hangin' offenses in Texas. This guy knew he'd hang and still made no move to get away or go heels against him.

Lowe said, "I ain't gonna draw. I saw you in Webber's Falls. I can't beat you. I guess I'll just take my chance with the Judge."

Hunter said "Put your hands on your head. I'm gonna come take that pistol from you; then we're goin' to visit the Sheriff." Lowe did as he was told. While he saddled his horse Hunter sent Donnie to get their horses. The three of them rode to the Sheriff's office together.

Once at the Sheriff's office they walked in and the Sheriff

said, "Finally caught one at home huh Frank? You let him wait long enough didn't ya? You been home for a week and I've seen him every evenin'."

Frank said, "He rented a house, he wasn't goin' anywhere." Frank unfolded the poster and handed it to the big burly Sheriff. "Can you wire the Wise County Sheriff and tell him I have his man and I need the reward. Lock him up till they come get him."

The Sheriff nodded and took a huge key ring from a wooden peg in the brick wall. He said, "In you go youngster." and pointed to one of the two cells he had in the back of the office. Lowe did exactly what he was told. Hunter told the Sheriff he'd come by tomorrow and see to the reward arrangements.

Lowe said from the cell "I admire your commitment Frank. Not many would have trailed me like that." Hunter looked at him to make sure he was serious then said, "I always figured a job worth startin' is a job worth finishin'. Let's see how much you admire me from the gallows Davey Boy. That'll tell the tale."

On the ride home Hunter told Donnie he had never caught a man that was so glad to get caught. They pulled into the farm and unsaddled the horses, put them in the corral with Liz's wagon team, and went to the barn to sleep. To Hunter's surprise there were two bunks made up in the barn with blankets and clean sheets. He said, "Just like the hotel in Ft. Smith." Hunter washed his stitches with alcohol from his saddlebag and pulled his jeans back on then pulled off his boots. They slept till Liz came in to feed the horses at sunup.

She said, "Breakfast is on the table."

Donnie and Hunter washed up at the pump in the corral. Donnie drew a bucket to take to the house. They went inside to the smell of grits and red eye gravy and coffee. Hunter ate his breakfast slowly. Still not used to eating in the morning, coffee was what he needed. He asked Donnie to saddle the horses after they ate. They needed to go see the sheriff. Donnie did as he was asked.

When Donnie was gone Liz asked Frank why hadn't he

married Marla before now. Hunter thought long before he spoke. He said, "Liz, I have been a hunter of men since Marla and I have been together. She has been a saloon girl longer than that. I don't know any other way of life. We had an obligation that took more money than I could have made here as a farmer or shopkeeper. We had an obligation, and we both went about makin' sure that obligation was fulfilled.

Liz asked, "What obligation would make you stay away from home for twenty years?"

Frank said, "Marla didn't tell you?"

Liz shook her head. "We had a daughter together nineteen years ago this September twenty-fifth. She is living in St. Louis with Marla's sister. We've been payin' her upbringing ever since. Her name is Becca and I haven't seen her since she was three weeks old."

Liz walked up and hugged Frank. She said, "Nineteen years is a long upbringin' Frank. You could stop now and live your days out right here on the farm with Marla. You could settle down before one of those outlaws kills you first."

Frank thought a moment and said, "It's too late for that now, Liz. It's all I know how to do. I am never as comfortable in a bed. I need to be out on the trail. I've been there all my life. I left here after Pop, and I haven't slept inside six months in the last twenty-four years combined. I really only like to sleep inside when it's cold outside. Even then I only do it some of the time. I can sleep out in the winter as long as I stay south of the Red River. Hell Marla's the same way. Her life has been spent in that saloon. She mothers those girls, births their babies, and looks out for their well-being. She wouldn't last here bein' a farm wife, feedin' the chickens and doin' the wash. She'd hate me in a year. I'd resent her for keepin' me home. Maybe when we get a bit older we'll give it a go, but for now we're still doin' our life's work, such as it is."

Frank kinda rubbed the place on his thigh where the stitches were. He said "These stitches gotta come out tonight they're itchin' me something awful."

Liz said, "I can take out stitches big brother."

Frank smiled, he liked the sound of that. He said, "I better wait for Marla. She likes to take every opportunity to torture me, besides I kinda gotta come out of my drawers to get to 'em.

Liz said, "Well I guess you'd better wait for Marla at that."

Donnie Came in and said, "We're all saddled up."

Frank told Liz, "See you in a bit Baby Sister." and off they went. Frank was happy Liz was back and okay even though she'd had a rough time of it with her husband, Frank thought she landed on her feet pretty well.

At the Sheriff's Office Hunter had a just tied his big gelding to the rail when the Sheriff came out and sat down in a rocker on the porch. He said, "Sit down Frank, let's talk a minute." Hunter did as the big man asked. The Sheriff went on. "I got a wire back from the Wise County Sheriff this morning. It seems you are going to have to take David Lowe to Decatur to get your reward. If you'd a brung him in dead, I could have identified him and they would'a wired the reward, but they want him hung in Decatur and the Sheriff there don't have no extra man to send after him. Now the only thing I can think to do is either you saddle up and deliver him to the Sheriff in Decatur, or take him out of town and shoot him and bring him back to be identified."

"Well shit" Hunter said under his breath. "I ain't gonna go out and murder him. I guess we'll pick him up in the morning and head to Decatur with him. I'll pay another night of room and board for him Sheriff if it's ok with you."

"Fine by me Frank. He's been eatin' my leftovers from home anyway. Keeps me from havin' to eat my Old Lady's dried out pot roast two nights in a row. Hell, I might pay you."

They rode up the street to the Three Doors for a cool beer. When they walked in Hunter looked at Marla and she knew. She walked over to the bar and asked flatly, "When are ya leavin'?"

"Tomorrow morning, We gotta take him to Decatur. Be back in a couple of weeks. I could just take him out and shoot him and be back by supper but I won't do that."

She said, "You'd better not."

21.– A Message Home.

Frank and Donnie spent the rest of the day getting ready to hit the trail. They cleaned the tools, filled the coffee bag, Donnie went to town and bought six cans of peaches and two boxes of shotgun shells.

Frank stressed to him, "If you leave for three days, pack like you won't be back for a year."

Donnie also went to the Bank and refilled his hatband. Frank refilled the oil and solvent bottles in his gun cleaning bag. They stowed everything in their saddlebags and washed up for supper.

Marla came out from town at about dusk; she had a basket in the buggy seat beside her. There were two full fried chickens in that basket. They made the rest of a feast from the pantry. The four of them ate and talked well into the night.

Liz told them she thought she'd have a house bought by the time they got back. Frank reminded her of the one just vacated by Lowe. It had a little corral and a tack shed. She could trade that wagon and team of Morgan geldings in for a nice buggy and a Quarter horse to pull it.

Marla looked pleased at the family gathered at the table and how they were getting along when she stopped the smiles with a somber thought, "Don't you get this young man killed Frank Hunter. He's got promise. I know you see yourself in him and he may be cut out for your work. I know you think it's too late for you, and it might well be, but it's not too late for Donnie. He's got a whole life ahead of him. Why don't you leave him here and go to Decatur alone?"

Frank sat there stunned for a second. He'd already accepted the kid as a partner and it never crossed his mind to leave him behind. Donnie was visibly upset and said, "I won't be stayin' here. I am Hunter's partner. If he goes I go. End of story." Frank gave Marla a little grin. She knew it before she said it but she had to say it anyway.

Marla knew in her heart that if Becca had been a boy there would have been no way Frank would've let her go with her sister, or anyone else. Marla would've quit the Three Doors and move out to this old farm house. Maybe Frank would have wound up in the sheriff's office or the Marshall's which moved down to Shreveport some years back, but Hunter would have kept a son. He'll keep this boy which he views as a son, too. In retrospect Marla couldn't find fault in what they'd done. She just remembered the long nights nineteen years ago she cried herself to sleep wondering if Becca was alright. She'd know for sure soon enough.

That night Marla took out Hunter's stitches. He didn't make it back out to the barn for some time.

The next morning dawned hot and sultry without a breath of breeze. Donnie and Hunter were up before the sun. "We'll have coffee and nothing else. Prob'ly still be in the bushes half the mornin' over that fried chicken." Hunter made coffee while Donnie saddled the horses and brought them to the house.

Liz and Marla got up and came out to see them off. Marla said, "Donnie I wish you'd stay here and help Liz get her things moved."

I'll move her stuff the day we get back. But I am goin' today."

Marla said, "You be careful then and watch Franks back."

Donnie said, "I will that's what I'm there for."

She looked at Frank, just as beautiful in her bath robe and her hair in a long braid as she was in her ball gown at the Three Doors, maybe more so, and said, "Frank you mind me now and watch that boy. I don't know how but I feel like he's special." Hunter nodded and kissed her long and deep. Then he mounted up and away they went. Donnie turned and waved twice.

Hunter just rode.

The railroad that ran through Texarkana in those days didn't go west. It came down from St. Louis across Arkansas and continued southwest to Dallas. It would have been so much easier to chain him up in the baggage car and ride the train one day to Decatur. On horseback makin' twenty five miles a day it would take eight days to get to Decatur. Hunter had packed an extra plate and spoon for Lowe, and hoped he liked Rabbit.

When they got to the Sheriff's office Hunter borrowed two pairs of cuffs from the Sheriff with the understanding that if they didn't come back, Hunter owed the county five dollars a pair for them. Hunter tried to pay for Lowes meals but the Sheriff told him that Lowe had paid the bill himself out of the money that was on him when was arrested, had paid for a telegram to his mother too. Hunter stopped in his tracks.

"Telegram? What'd it say?" The Sheriff told him it just said he had done some bad things and that he was being taken from Texarkana to Decatur to stand trial. Hunter was furious. Now he'd have to watch every bush for two hundred miles.

Donnie got Lowe's horse and rig from the livery he paid his bill and headed back to the Sheriff's office. There was a train unloading at the station and Donnie thought, "Someday I'm gonna go somewhere on that train just to say I did." Just then a pretty young lady stepped down from the train and opened a parasol against the hot morning sun and looked at Donnie. Donnie tipped his Stetson and smiled; she dipped a little curtsy and smiled back. He headed up the street to the Sheriff's thinkin'; "Yep, gotta ride that train."

They got Lowe mounted on his horse and chained with a cuff from the saddle horn to each wrist. Hunter didn't think he could run too far like that, and if he did he couldn't get off the horse. They said their goodbyes to the Sheriff and headed East. They passed the pretty girl in a hired surrey half way out of town Donnie tipped his hat again. She smiled and waved this time. Hunter just nodded.

22.– Chris Lowe

Chris Lowe worked in the stockyards in Ft. Worth Texas. He worked long hours and made a livin' for himself and his Mother until last June, when Mother had passed away. It had been a year since she'd been gone and Chris had been thinking of selling the little house and traveling around a while. Why not, there was nothing to keep him here.

The funeral had been nice. Lots of friends and neighbors turned out. David was even here for the service. He didn't stay long though, he seldom did. He stopped at a saloon for a beer on the way home and shot the breeze with a buddy from the stock yards and went home. Not too much of a carouser was Chris Lowe.

He walked up the steps and onto the porch before he saw the telegram there pinched in the clothespin Mother had tacked to the door for notes and such. He opened the telegram and knew what he had to do at once.

The next morning he went to a little office of a man he knew that bought houses to rent out. He sold Mother's house, furniture clothespin and all for six-hundred dollars.

He went back to the house for the last time and packed a carpetbag full of clothes.

He went to a livery and bought a horse and rig. He hadn't needed one before. If he went somewhere he hired a horse. He was leaving now for good.

He stopped by the stockyards and told his boss he'd have to find someone else to open and close the damned gates; he quit.

He headed out for Dallas before ten in the morning. He stopped in Dallas at around three in the afternoon and bought a few camp items; bedroll, coffee pot, a quarter side of bacon, some beans, and a rifle, a Winchester. He headed out. He knew where he was going; he hoped he had enough time.

Chris was headed to Mount Pleasant, Texas. He knew there

wasn't a mountain there and he doubted if it was pleasant but that was where he'd set David free. He'd do it for Mother. They would head west. Surely this man wouldn't follow them more than a week or so. They could shake him by then. Obviously Chris Lowe didn't know Frank Hunter.

23.– Mount Pleasant

He pulled into Mount Pleasant, Texas late the next afternoon. The sun was hot and he'd forgotten to buy a canteen. He'd been drinking from streams along the way, but they were warm. One farmer drew him a cool bucket from his well and he'd drunk four or five dippers full. He thanked the farmer and went his way.

Chris wasn't a lawless man. He was a decent law abiding kind of fellow. He just couldn't let Dave go to the gallows so soon after losing Mother. He could only stand so much grief right now. He reigned up at the first saloon and ordered a beer. He hoped it was cool while he waited. It was nice and cool. He drained it and ordered another. He asked the barman if he could drink it in one of the rockers out on the porch. The bartender said "Sheriff don't allow no drinkin' in the street. A'course the porch ain't in the street. If ya step off the porch with it he'll lock ya up for the night if he catches ya.

Chris allowed that he wouldn't, "It's just one of them rockers looked pretty good right about now."

He went outside and sat in a rocker in the shade: sipped his beer and waited.

Hunter didn't like traveling with David Lowe near as much as he liked trailing him. He never stopped talking about something. Even Donnie was ready for him to shut up. Hunter knew his game though: he was tryin' to keep them engaged and not alert. Hunter heard one out of five words he said but he was fully aware of his surroundings. Five years behind enemy lines teaches you awareness. Hunter never forgot. Finally, Hunter wheeled around and said "Lowe, this paper says dead or alive. I ain't gonna kill a chained up man, but I will break your nose with a pistol barrel if you don't shut up. Look in my eyes and see if I'm lyin'."

Dave looked into Hunter's eyes and saw that he wasn't. He guessed that the story of how he had rode a riverboat from New Orleans to Minneapolis could wait till morning. Chris would have to think on his feet if he was gonna get this done. If he got the telegram at all.

They camped by a little creek that first night. Hunter told Donnie, "One of us'll have to keep watch all night, since he sent that telegram, there may be someone comin' to set him free. It would be a mistake because if they come with a gun I'll kill 'em and that'll be on ol' Davie here's mind and conscience right up until they cinch the knot."

Hunter opened the right hand cuff on the saddle horn and just said "Get down and unsaddle your horse." He fumbled through it but he got it off alright. Hunter told him, "Lay it down where you wanna sit." After he got sat down Hunter attached the free cuff to the left stirrup. He didn't think Dave could get far dragging a saddle behind his back on both arms. He could still eat and move around he was just slow moving. They ate jerky from Hunter's saddlebag and canned peaches. Donnie even gave Dave a can. They were hard to eat with the spoon but he got it done and thanked Donnie for the treat. He hoped the kid didn't get hurt when Chris caught up to them.

Hunter took the first watch and told Donnie to go to sleep as soon as it was dark. He said, "Sleep now and I'll wake you up when the moon's straight up."

Donnie did as he was told, Hunter started another pot of coffee.

Dave said, "We gonna eat jerky every night? I had you pegged as a live off the land sort of man, rabbits and owls and shit like that. The peaches kinda took me by surprise."

Hunter growled, "The peaches are Donnies idea and he gives 'em to whoever he wants. I expect you'll be eatin' beans in the Mount Pleasant jail tomorrow night. Your little telegram has made me rethink this whole trip. I'll put you up in jails every night that I can. Now shut up and go to sleep."

Dave said I have to relieve myself before I go to sleep." and held his hands out to be unlocked. Hunter said, "Be quiet draggin' that saddle you'll wake Donnie up."

Hunter woke Donnie up about one in the morning as close as he could tell. He came right out of it and jumped to his feet. Hunter told him "Stoke that fire up it's not even chilly but it'll help keep you awake. If you need more coffee make some I finished that pot."

Donnie nodded and Hunter laid down closer to them than Donnie had. He'd sleep but not soundly. He'd sleep tomorrow night in Mount Pleasant. He dozed.

Hunter heard Donnie fumbling with the coffee pot and opened his eyes and the sky was just startin to lighten up. He sat up and Donnie said "I didn't mean to wake you Hunter. I was just startin' the coffee."

Hunter said, "You didn't, it's time I got up anyway. He been quiet all night?"

Donnie nodded.

Hunter said, "He sure sleeps sound for someone who's gonna swing in ten or twelve days. The trial in Decatur's just gonna be a formality. He killed their constable with several witnesses in the bank. He'll be convicted in twenty minutes."

Hunter kicked him in the foot and said, "If you want Coffee you'd better sit up. We're leavin' as soon as I see the sun."

Lowe sat up and said, "What's for breakfast gents, Bacon and eggs, Biscuits and gravy, Eggs Benedict?"

Donnie just said, "Coffee."

They headed West along the road that wound its way across the North edge of Texas about thirty miles South of Red River. The day passed rather quietly, but Hunter could tell Lowe was tensing up and watchin' the bushes. If they could just get to Mount Pleasant, they could relax tonight and get some sleep.

They came into Mount Pleasant just before dusk. It was a sleepy little one street farm community. They rode the length of the main street past the feed store and general store and hardware store that were both closed and dark. There were three or four men sitting on the porch of the saloon drinkin' cool mugs of beer. Hunter thought one of those might go down good after supper.

He walked into the Sheriff's office. There was a big coal oil lantern hangin in the middle of the room. The Sheriff was a big burly man. He got up and Hunter handed him the poster that was getting' pretty worn. He said, "I'm Frank Hunter, I'm takin' this man to Decatur for trial and I'd appreciate it if you keep him in jail tonight so me and my pard can get some sleep. I'll be happy to pay for his board."

The Sheriff looked at the poster and said, "Bring him in we'll get him locked up and talk over the particulars." He stuck out a bearlike paw and said I'm Ed Kilman, Sheriff of Titus County.

Hunter and Donnie got him down and took him inside each of them holdin the free end of a cuff. Hunter took the other end of the cuffs off and Sheriff Killman locked him in a cell in the back room of the office.

He looked at Hunter and said, "There's still a café open up the street. If you gents go eat there and pay for a plate for him they'll bring it down to him. I already have a prisoner in there so I don't have to pay for a jailer extra so I don't need nothin' from you Mister Hunter. You gents go have a bite and get some sleep; we'll watch him for ya tonight."

They went outside and looked up the street just as a Deputy was lightin' the lamps along the boardwalk.

Hunter told Donnie, "Go put the horses up while I rent us a room, then we'll go to the café."

Donnie headed of to the livery with the horses while hunter found a boarding house that had one room with two beds left.

Hunter rented it and headed over to the livery to help with the gear. Two saddle bags, two rifles, and two shotguns were a little much for one man to carry up the street.

They carried their gear over to the cafe and leaned the long guns up in a corner while they ordered. The special was roast beef with potatoes, gravy, and green beans. Donnie and Hunter both had the special and sent the same to the jail for Lowe. They finished their meal and decided they were both too tired to get a beer. They went to the boarding house and turned in.

Chris Lowe sat there in the shade sipping a beer when the big man on the gelding and a kid who looked nineteen years old came through town with his brother in irons. They reigned up at the Sheriff's office. David's eyes found his at once. They went up the street. No one noticed the man on the horse looked almost exactly like the man sippin' a beer on the porch of the saloon. Both had the same eyes, and the same four day stubble on their face. The gambler on the horse's clothes were a bit fancier that the stockyard hand's clothes, but their faces were very similar. The big man went inside while the kid sat outside with Dave. The big man came back, out and they all went inside. When they came back out they went their separate ways one to the livery one to the boarding house. After they did their business they went to the café.

When they'd been in the café for a bit, Chris Lowe untied his horse from the rail and took him to the livery. He paid one day in advance. He told the liveryman, "Give him some grain he's got a hard trip tomorrow. Can I leave my gear here with my saddle?

The liveryman said he didn't care but he wasn't responsible for it. "If it's gone in the mornin' it's on you." Chris nodded. He went back to the saloon and got another beer and waited. When the boy and the big man came out of the café they went straight to the boarding house.

After they went inside Chris got up from his rocker, he went inside and got a fresh mug and went back out to the porch. It was only about his sixth beer since he got into town but when he got outside he started to stagger. He took the beer with him and went up the street toward the Sheriff's office. The closer he got the more he staggered. He was almost to the office which stood on the corner of a large lot that housed the courthouse when the deputy that lit all the lanterns gently took him by the arm and started leading him toward the Sheriff's Office. He wasn't rude or rough just firm enough to let you know he was gonna get you there, so you might as well come along quietly. Chris had never been arrested before but he figured this was prob'ly one of the better lawmen.

Inside the jail the Sheriff said, "What's this Charlie?"

"Found him staggering up the street." Chris was still holding the mug.

The Sheriff said, "Drink up son. You're spending the night in the clink here with ol' Charlie." Chris turned the mug up and drained it and ol' Charlie led him into the back room and put him in the same cell as his brother.

David didn't look up. He was workin' on a plate of roast beef and mashed potatoes he looked pretty happy about. Chris sat down on the opposite bunk, when Dave looked up he said. "You gotta get your own dinner this guy never eats." He grinned and they hugged. Dave said what are you doin' in jail brother? I'm the bad apple." Chris replied "Gettin' you free brother. I have a plan."

When the sun came up the next morning 'ol Charlie came back and said, "You ready to go beer drinker?" He got up and said, "I sure am. I am sorry 'bout last night Deputy it won't happen again." Charlie said, "That'd be best, Mister." Charlie locked the cell and out they went. He went outside and down the street to the livery. He got the horse out. The liveryman said "Your all paid up, be careful out on the trail, Mister." He gathered up the gear. The rifle and bacon and beans would come in handy for the next week. David Lowe rode out of Mount Pleasant headed north. He was wearin' his brother's clothes and ridin' his brother's horse. Smiling at the way it worked out.

Last night Chris told him he had it all figured out down to how many days since he'd shaved. He had a horse in the livery a roan. He'd left a rifle and some gear in a carpetbag there. There was some bacon and beans. "Head out north, ride upstream in the red river for a long ways and meet me outside Terral in a week. We'll go out west and be clear of this business." David knew better. Hunter had trailed him across the Nations, twice. He wouldn't give up in a week.

24. – Fool Me Once

Donnie woke Hunter up at around six thirty in the morning. They went downstairs to some pretty good hotcakes with butter and maple syrup. Donnie went to the livery and collected the horses while Hunter had another cup of coffee. They loaded up and headed to the jail. When they got there Hunter got the cuffs out of his saddlebag and they went inside to collect Lowe. Sheriff Kilman was just putting his coffee pot on the stove when they walked in. He said, "Mornin' boys. Come to gather up yer belongin's?"

"We have in fact." Hunter answered back. He genuinely liked this big Sheriff.

The Sheriff said, "Ol' Charlie didn't hear a peep out of him last night. I peeked in when I came in and he was still sawin' logs." The big man grabbed the keys off the peg and they went back. He was still asleep alright. Sheriff Kilman unlocked the cell and kicked the bunk and said "Time to get up youngster, your ride is here."

The man on the Bunk rolled over and said, "Mornin' Sheriff I am sorry about last night. I had a few too many beers." He looked a lot like Lowe, he was wearin' his clothes, but the voice was all wrong. Frank looked at the Sheriff and said lock the cell back. The Sheriff slammed the cell door with a bang so loud it woke up the other prisoner in the other cell that was waitin' on a meeting with his own hangman.

They went into the outer office. Hunter said,"I bet a hundred dollars that man in there is David Lowe's brother. He sent a telegram from Texarkana to Fort Worth three days ago. He's had enough time to get here from there.

Sheriff Kilman looked at Hunter and said, "I can't hold this man in jail." Hunter said "Why not? He helped a prisoner escape. Surely you can hold him on something."

The Sheriff said, "I'll ask the judge when he comes in but I think all he's done is drink beer on the street and trade his clothes for some fancier ones. He didn't hit a guard or even give a false statement."

Hunter said, "Ed, If you could give me twelve hours before you turn him loose I would really appreciate it. I need to do some thinkin' before he hits the road." The Sheriff rubbed his chin and said, "Frank I'll keep him here till eight p.m. without tellin' the judge or anyone else. After eight he'll be in the wind. I hope you catch your man Hunter."

Donnie and Hunter went back out to the horses and Hunter put the cuffs back in his saddlebag. They mounted up and went to the livery and dropped Lowe's horse and rig back off and paid one more day's keep on him. Hunter told the hostler, "If no one comes for him this evenin' he's yours." Hunter got down and stooped over and picked up Lowe's horse's hind foot and looked at the shoe Bernie had put on in Broken Bow; he smiled, It had a BF stamped into it. Hunter and Donnie rode out of town headed South at a gallop.

David Lowe rode Chris' horse upstream in the red river, keeping to the shallows. Chris' horse didn't like the deep water. Dave had to spur him pretty good to get him to cross the river channel when the river went around a bend. All the while he was thinking Hunter couldn't track him through five miles of knee deep running water if he was an Apache. Sure as he was he kept up the pace Chris' horse was lathered up. He'd have to give him a break soon. He'd stop and let him have a little drink as soon as he found a rock ledge he could get out of this water on and not leave a track. He thought about Chris. How he'd come up with this plan. He smiled thinkin' about Hunter and the kid goin' to get him and he was long gone. He watered the horse and got out of the river on the south side. He headed Southwest at an easy lope. He could almost smell those New Mexico Mountains Chris talked about. Still all the while there was an itch in his mind. He didn't think Hunter would be this easy to slip.

After a few miles Hunter slowed it to an easier gait. Donnie followed along and watched Hunter. He occasionally shook his head, then he'd laugh. Donnie could tell Hunter was furious. After a bit he spurred the big gelding and they raced away again he was acting different than Donnie had ever seen him act.

Hunter turned it over and over in his mind. The telegram had made him not want to camp along the trail for fear of a night attack, so he had taken Lowe into Mount Pleasant to the jail for safekeepin'. He was safe alright, only in the mornin', the Deputy just let him out and kept his brother who had gotten arrested for public drunk. Actually the man hadn't broken any laws except the public drinkin'. "Dammit!" Hunter screamed at himself in his head. "They fooled you." They wouldn't do it again.

Hunter rode north toward the Red River at an alternately easy and fast pace trying to keep the horses as fresh as he could. They could have a long day. He just rode; he didn't talk to Donnie or even look around to see if the kid was still there. He had miles to make up and decisions to make. If Lowe got back into the territories he would not be that hard to find; he'd done it before, twice. Hunter just needed to see if that was where he was going before his brother got out of the hoosegow at eight o'clock.

They reigned up where the trail crossed the Red River. Hunter dismounted and walked downstream along the south bank studying the sandy riverbank as he went. After two hundred yards he turned around and studied it all the way back to the road. Donnie said, "What are you doing Hunter, Lowe's gettin' farther away while you look for frogs in the river."

Hunter paid no attention. He just said, "Get down and you might learn something." He started upstream studying the riverbank. Donnie followed along ten feet back. It didn't take long to find what he was looking for.

There was a horse track where the hind leg slipped a little on the sloped surface of the river bank. The bottom of the track was still damp from being turned up. It would have been dry in two hours. This was fresh, or at least less than two hours old. Hunter walked back to the road and mounted up and crossed the river. He rode upstream a quarter of a mile and saw nothing. He came back to the road and crossed back to the South side. He dismounted and did something that made Donnie's jaw drop. He got out the coffee pot and started building a fire in the middle of the hard packed road bed. Donnie looked on with amazement. Hunter got the coffee going and sat down cross-legged in the road and waited for the coffee with the two cups sittin' in the dirt waiting with him. Donnie sat down a said nothing. He could see on Hunter's face he was working up to his explanation.

Finally he looked at Donnie and said, "Fool me once, Shame on me. They fooled me good but I'm trying to not let it happen again. I'm sure that drunk in the jail is Lowe's brother. I think he wasn't as drunk as he let on. He was in Mount Pleasant waitin' on us. He figured we would put Lowe up in the jail after the telegram. He was right. We couldn't keep up the watches with only two of us. Now what I have to decide is this. Will Lowe go back into the Nations after I've already caught him there he knows I can do it again? I think he will join back up with his brother somewhere West of here and flee. Probably leave this part of the world for the rest of their lives."

Donnie said, "That's why you looked at the shoe. We're gonna trail the brother to Lowe aren't we?"

Hunter nodded and sipped his coffee. He poured another

cup. "He won't get sprung from jail till eight, we have time for another cup then we gotta get busy." They had another cup then they got up and Donnie stomped out the little fire. They headed back to Mount Pleasant at a trot.

25. Back on the Hunt

Hunter and Donnie sat in the Shadows behind a one room Church you could see the jail and all the way down to the livery. The clock on the courthouse struck eight and five minutes later Lowe's brother walked out the front door of the jail. Hunter had hidden their horses on the other side of the building and he and Donnie sat in some bushes eating a can of peaches. Brother Lowe (as Hunter now thought of him) walked nice and easy down to the livery and pounded on the closed barn door.

The hostler opened the door in a minute clearly not happy to be bothered this late at night. Chris said, "I'm here to get my horse. A big guy with a kid left it here night before last."

The liveryman said, "Your rig's on the rail there and your horse is in the third stall. He's fed and ready."

Chris asked, "What's the damage?"

The liveryman said, "The big guy paid today before he left and said if no one came for him he was mine. I'm not too happy to see you. I already had your saddle sold if it was here tomorrow."

"Well sorry to disappoint you ol' timer. I gotta take him out tonight."

The hostler said, "I'm closed for the day. Saddle him yourself. I'll close up after you're gone." Brother Lowe saddled his new mount. He could tell from looking this was a better horse than he'd bought in Ft. Worth. He tipped the livery man a wave and headed west out of town.

Donnie stood up as if to leave right then, but Hunter told him to sit back down. "We won't leave for another half hour or so. Let's go get a meal and then we'll head out." They went back to the café and ordered stew and cornbread when Sheriff Kilman walked in.

He said, "I thought I saw you boys come in here. Did you find out what you needed to know?"

Hunter nodded and said, "Did you get his name" I bet his last name is Lowe isn't it?"

The Sheriff said, "Yup it sure was, Christopher Lowe, Ft. Worth, Texas. He had three hundred dollars on him. I don't know where he went after I turned him out, but he didn't seem to be in no hurry."

Hunter said, "I know we watched him from up the street. He just saddled up and headed out West down the main street. We'll follow him after we eat. He won't leave the road in the dark and I don't want him to see us till he meets his brother." The Sheriff sat there and ate dinner with them. After the meal they walked out on the porch and Hunter shook his hand and said, "I may be back here in a few days with ol' Dave over his saddle. I have a feelin' with two of them he'll fight this time. I'll bring him here to put in for the reward. I like this café."

Sheriff Kilman said "I'll see you then Frank." He shook Donnie's hand and they were off.

They rode at an easy pace there was plenty of moonlight to see the road and they didn't want to ride up on Chris in the dark. He prob'ly wouldn't get ten feet off the trail to make his camp. After a couple of hours they topped a ridge and saw a campfire about a quarter mile ahead. Hunter stopped and turned back and dismounted below the crest of the ridge. They unsaddled the horses and tied them out in a grassy spot. They walked back to the top and looked down on Chris Lowe. He was sittin' by the side of the road. It looked like he was drinkin' coffee. "He'll sleep tight." Hunter whispered. "He thinks we're in the nations lookin' for David. I am almost positive he'll meet up with Dave tomorrow, and they'll light out, prob'ly West. If we don't catch 'em here we'll be in for a long ride."

David Lowe sat by his fire. The beans were almost done and smellin' pretty good. He was so hungry he almost ate 'em as soon as they got soft enough to chew. He waited though, he thought to himself it's been since last night since I've eaten what's another hour. He just sat there watchin' southeast. He knew no one could find where he came out of the river. He also knew no one could track him in the dark. He knew Frank Hunter wouldn't give up easily, so he watched and waited for the beans to cook.

He'd set up his camp about a quarter mile south of the road between Terrell and Dallas. He hadn't gone into town he skirted around the South side of Terrell and picked this spot around dusk. He saw a house on the south edge of Terrell that had eight sides. It was a perfect octagon with rifle holes in every wall. It was scarred up from the Indian attacks it had survived. It still stood there as defiant as the day it was built. Dave thought to himself. "I'll have to remember that when we get to New Mexico. That's a hell of an idea."

He was about four miles West of Terrell. On a little ridge but the Mesquite bushes hid his fire from the road. When the beans were done he ate most of them. Two bowls full and thought to himself "The rest of those will make a pretty good breakfast." He covered the pot with his bowl and turned in. Chris should be there tomorrow evening. "We'll have to eat beans again. I'll start 'em earlier tomorrow."

Hunter nudged Donnie's elbow well before sunrise. Down the hill Chris was stoking the fire up and startin' a pot of coffee. They sat and watched as he went about packin' up while the coffee brewed. After it was done Brother Lowe sat down and drank two cups. He was relaxed, why wouldn't he be. He was just a law abidin' traveler havin' his morning coffee. Hunter and Donnie moved back down the bluff. The sun was coming up behind them and Hunter didn't want Chris to catch their silhouettes in the light. Hunter told Donnie to gather some sticks. "After he rides off we'll make our own coffee before we leave. He needs to get a mile or two ahead. We'll close on him this evening." Chris rode off about ten minutes later after he topped the next ridge Donnie got the fire goin' and brewed coffee.

The day passed pretty unevenfully. Every couple of miles Hunter would get down and find the BF in the hoof print to make sure Chris hadn't turned off. In the late afternoon Hunter spurred the big gelding into a trot. They kept that up until they topped the hill overlooking Terrell. They went into town at a walk, and Hunter reigned up at the first saloon. They tied their horses there to the rail and walked around the corner. Hunter told Donnie, "His horse is tied up at the general store." Donnie was amazed again at the talents of this man. He had had a look at the street all of about twenty seconds and spotted a horse that wasn't even his.

They waited around the corner Hunter checking every now and then at the general store. He came out after a few minutes with a burlap sack in one hand. He tied the sack of provisions to the saddle horn and off he went again, still west. Hunter told Donnie, "We'll wait a few minutes to let him clear town." After he did they stopped in the same store and got some cold food including some canned peaches. There would be no fire tonight.

After the store they rode out west. Hunter told Donnie, "He won't ride far the way he tied that sack on. If he was goin' any distance he would have packed that stuff away in the saddlebags. I would guess he's gonna meet ol' Dave this evening." After they left town they kept their slow pace for about an hour till Hunter saw where Chris turned right and headed south into the Mesquites. There was a small piece of cloth tied to a limb. It had to be the mark David had left. Chris should have taken it down but Hunter saw the tracks first anyway. "Lazy outlaws," Hunter thought to himself.

Hunter and Donnie kept going west for another couple of

miles till Hunter found the spot in the road he liked. It had a big tree right in a bend in the road, perfect. He reigned up and they walked into the mesquites a bit. Hunter made sure to warn Donnie about those damned Mesquite thorns. "You didn't have these in Arkansas or the Indian Territory. These are purely a Texas thing. The thorns get up to three inches long and they're tough as a nail. If you step on one right it'll go through the sole of your boot."

They tied the horses out in a grassy patch and came back to the road. They sat down and had a meal of jerky, saltine crackers, and canned peaches. Hunter was gettin' used to the peaches. They turned in as soon as it was dark. They were off the road about thirty feet but no one was gonna pass un-noticed.

Chris Lowe rode into the camp only to be greeted by the muzzle of his own rifle. He said, "Put that damned thing down." He dismounted and gave his little brother a hug. He said, "Damn it's good to see you in the wide open, Brother. I think we gave 'em all the slip. Now in the morning we'll head west and keep headin' west till we're out of Texas. Up in them mountains we'll be fine. I got you a pistol at the general store. I also got a belt and holster. I smell them beans and I'm about to cave in, I'm so hungry, Let's eat."

David said, "They're ready, tomorrow when we leave, you not only get your rifle back but your clothes and your damned horse."

Chris said, "I don't blame you on the horse. He's a little weak on the spirit compared to yours." They had supper and enjoyed each other's company. It was the first time they'd had time to talk since Mother'd passed. Then neither of them felt much like talking. They ate, had coffee, and went to sleep. Chris thinking of New Mexico. He wanted to see those mountains. David was wondering how long Hunter would look in the Nations before he came this way? If they had a week head start on him he'd never catch up. They would grow beards and change clothes. By the time they got there he wouldn't look like the poster anymore. He went to sleep thinking of a new name.

Hunter woke Donnie two hours before the sun came up and went over it with him again. He'd done it last night and Donnie knew his part. Hunter was really serious about not gettin' fooled again. Hunter started again, "I want you behind that big tree. Jack a round into the chamber of your rifle and let the hammer down to the half cock notch, then wait. Stay hid until you hear me talk. When you hear me, come out just enough to shoot that rifle around the right side of that tree. I want you to pay attention to Brother Chris. He'll be back on his own horse. He'll prob'ly have his own clothes on again. I don't think David has a gun. He didn't have one in jail, and Brother Chris didn't have one when he was in Terrell. I'm gonna hunker down in the Mesquites here, and when they get about twenty yards up the trail I will step out and try to take him to Decatur. They'll fight, I'm sure. You look to Brother Chris. If he jerks iron you take him down. I'll be lookin' to Dave." They took their places and waited.

Chris woke David up earlier than Dave was used to gettin' up under good circumstances. He said,"We need to get goin'. No coffee this morning." Chris had his own clothes back, and was busy packin' his less desirable horse. David got up and rolled up his blanket and started getting ready to head out. He saddled his horse and about the time the Eastern sky started to brighten up they started pickin' their way through the Mesquites toward the road.
They hit the road and David said, "You left the flag hangin' there? Ol' Frank would'a known right where to look if he wasn't in the nations lookin' for me." They turned West in the growing light.
"New Mexico or Bust." Chris said. David just nodded.

Donnie heard the horses coming up the road, but dared not

look. He had his orders and he wouldn't let Hunter Down. They were still a quarter mile out. It seemed like hours to Donnie as they closed the gap. Hunter stepped out of the Mesquites and said. "Dave, I'm still gonna take you to Decatur for the killin' of the constable." Donnie cocked the hammer of his '73 and aimed around the right side of the tree and put the front sight right on Brother Chris' chest.

"Frank Hunter!" David exclaimed. "I knew we couldn't shake you that easy. I tried to talk myself into it but I never really bought it. This is my brother Chris. Sorry about the way we fooled you back in Mount Pleasant." Hunter could see the new gun belt and colt hangin' there. Dave said, "Frank we were just headin' to the mountains up in New Mexico. I'm afraid I ain't got the time to go to Decatur right now. Will you give us the road?" Frank shook his head. Donnie could see Chris' hand inchin' toward the butt of his rifle. But he hadn't touched it yet. To Donnie, time seemed to have slowed down, everything that happened in the next thirty seconds ticked by with exquisite clarity. "Sorry Frank I can't go in and swing."

Hunter said. "Dave it's down to fight or flee. If you flee I'll shoot you. Your brother will prob'ly get away. If you stand and fight and he pulls that rifle he'll go down with you. He didn't kill anybody, but you'll kill him just like you pulled the trigger yourself. Think about it."

Dave looked at Chris for a second then he said, "Chris ride out. Go to New Mexico for both of us. I won't be shot in the back running, and this big guy's too fast to beat." Chris walked his horse forward about ten feet then he grabbed the rifle he one handed cocked it and started to point it at Hunter when Donnie shot him he had leaned over to the left and Donnie's shot took him in the right shoulder. The bullet went all the way through, he dropped the rifle and fell from the saddle. Donnie cocked the rifle just in time to see Dave clear leather. Hunter watched as Lowe's gun came out of the holster then his hands were a blur. He gave Dave a head start and shot him twice before he could cock his piece.

Donnie walked around the tree just in time to step on the rifle Chris was tryin' to pick up left handed. He said "It's over Mister."

Chris looked up at Hunter and said, "He was my brother, I had to try." Hunter tore the back of Chris' shirt open and said "I know you did, I knew you would two days ago. I'm glad you ducked when you did. You didn't have comin' what your brother did. Now you can go on to New Mexico after you mend in Terrell for a spell. Now let's get this bleedin' stopped.

Donnie had been getting ol' Dave ready to go back. He said "He's got two hundred and fifty dollars in his shirt pocket."

Chris told them, "That was his half of the money Mother's house brought when I sold it the other day."

Hunter took it from Donnie and handed it back to Chris He said "He won't be needin' it." Hunter continued to apply pressure to the wounds. The front was almost stopped, and the back was slowin' down. Hunter told him "I had a wound just like this once. Took it all winter to mend. You don't want to be out in the cold tryin' to heal a wound like this. You'll be recovered by the time winter rolls around though. You should take your brother's horse and saddle. They're both better than yours." Hunter sat across from Chris and looked him in the eye and said "Chris, I want you to know that I am sorry for what I had to do to your brother. He killed a man in Decatur while he was robbin' the bank. He pulled the poster from his pocket and showed him the picture. You grow a beard or someone is gonna think it's you. You got lucky. If Donnie had been practicin' more with that rifle your brother would have killed you too. I know that's hard to hear but if you think about it you'll agree. I usually sell all the valuables of a bounty before I take 'em in but you can have anything he had that you want."

They got David Lowe loaded onto Brother Chris' horse and helped Chris onto David's horse. He had his rifle and supplies he didn't want the pistol, Donnie would wind up with it in a cross draw rig. They headed back East to Terrell, six of the quietest miles Hunter could remember riding.

25. Headed Home

They left Chris Lowe standing in front of the Doc's office in Terrell, and kept up a steady pace all day. They made camp early in the evening on a ridge and took Dave off his horse downwind. They took the horses to a creek on the north side of the bluff and let them water for a while. They tied them out in some grass and hunted. They had two fat cottontails in a few minutes, and a few minutes later they were fryin'. Hunter Said, "Donnie, I think I'm gonna just call you Don from now on. You've held up your end of everything we've done over the past month or so. You saved my life twice and acted like a man in everything I've had you do. I think Donnie is a boy's name. I don't think you're a boy anymore." Donnie hadn't even given his name any thought but now that it was said, he liked the idea. Hunter continued "I never wanted a partner out here. I always did alright by myself. I'd be dead now if it weren't for you and I do appreciate it. I have to ask you again if you think livin' out of a saddlebag, eatin' rabbits and squirrels every night is really what you want. We could still find that ranch job for you. You have a start now. That's what I promised you when you sat on that rock west of Webber's Falls. I guess what I'm sayin' is, I want you to stay on as my partner if that's what you want to do. If you don't I'll help you find a job near Texarkana. It's up to you Don."

Don Thought for a moment then looked Hunter in the eye and said, "I want to stay on with you. I have reasons if you wanna hear 'em." Hunter Sat down with the canvas bag that held his gun oil and brushes on the trail.

He started breakin' down his Colts and said, "I'm all ears Don." Don stared into the fire for a second then started. "I owe you my life, but that debt's paid back I figure. I want to stay on because even though you don't talk much, or listen much I have learned more from you in the last six weeks than I have learned in the rest of my life combined. I admire the way you always seem to know what's right and wrong. I admire the way you see everything at a glance and I hope to learn that from you too. There are things I can still learn from you and I'd like to hang around and learn 'em if you don't mind."

Hunter looked up from his guns while Don turned the rabbit quarters over in the skillet and said, "I'd be proud to teach you what I can. I've always had a kind of sense when trouble's coming, but most of the observation I learned in the War. Old Sergeant O'Malley always told me I couldn't fight what I couldn't see, so I see everything I can.

Don nodded, "So it's settled then?"

Hunter said, "As far as I'm concerned it is. When we get home we need to go buy some lumber and a stove and add you a room out at the barn. A man needs his own place. It'll give us something to keep us busy till we head out again." Don put the rabbit pieces on the plate and started to get the coffee goin'. They ate rabbit for supper like they had it seemed like a hundred times, and there would a thousand more till they quit this trail life, or they quit makin' rabbits. After they had eaten and were sippin coffee while the fire died down Don asked, "Why don't you want me at the house?" and grinned.

Hunter looked at him and thought about Marla in the morning wearin' one of his shirts and said, "Like I said sometimes a man needs his own place."

They slept on the side of the road that night without worry. They had their man, they were headed home. This adventure was over but Don went to sleep thinking of the next poster and where it would take them. Hunter went to sleep hopin' Chris Lowe would be alright. He was lucky Don had the job covering him. Don would have had no trouble takin' Dave off the draw but Hunter didn't want to put him there just yet. If Hunter had been covering Chris, he'd be coyote shit by now. Hunter slept the half sleep of a man who'd spent his life in wild lands with less than hospitable neighbors, still it was the best he'd slept since they sat out on this trip. They were still three or four days from home depending on Sheriff Kilman in Mount Pleasant.

They pulled into Mount Pleasant around Noon the next day. They pulled up in front of the Sheriff's Office and went inside to a startled Sheriff Kilman who was obviously nappin' in his chair. Hunter said, "Sorry Ed, didn't mean to interrupt your thinkin' there. I need you to come confirm this bounty, if you would." The big Sheriff got up and stretched and ambled out on the porch. Hunter handed him the poster and grabbed a handful of Dave's hair and lifted his head so the Sheriff could get a good look.

Kilman said, " Did'ja have to kill his brother?"

Don said, "He took a bullet to the shoulder but he'll be okay. We left him at the Doc's in Terrell."

The Sheriff said, "Good I kinda liked that guy. I don't think he would'a done that for anyone but his brother." Hunter nodded his agreement.

Hunter asked, "Where do ya want me to take him Ed? He's drawin' stares and flies out here in the street." The Sheriff pointed them to the undertakers out on the east edge of town. Hunter said, "We'll go get him taken care of and put the horses up and I'll buy your lunch Ed. I told ya I like that café." It was agreed they would meet for lunch at the café in forty five minutes. They took Dave to the undertakers and told him that ol' Dave needed the "County Special". They went to the livery and sold Chris' saddle Hunter had decided to keep Chris' roan mare for Liz's buggy horse. This animal was suited to a buggy more than a saddle anyway. He got twenty for the saddle and gave Don his ten. He said, "Here ya go pard, your half of the spoils." The went to the boarding house and checked into two rooms. They stowed their saddlebags and long guns, and headed for lunch. On the way to lunch Hunter spied a barber shop with a sign that said Baths One Dollar. He told Don he was gonna buy a suit of clothes and head over there after lunch. Don thought that was a great idea.

They met Ed Kilman and had a chicken fried steak, mashed potatoes and gravy, and cornbread. Hunter said, "I won't need supper now. The Sheriff told them he had wired off to Decatur and the voucher should be back in an hour or two. Hunter said, "I'm gonna get a shave, and a bath, and a change of drawers when we leave here.

The big man said "A change of drawers is a good thing as long as you don't just change with ol' Donnie here." They all had a chuckle.

Hunter said, "We'll check back with you before the Bank closes Ed."

He said, "I'll see you then Frank."

They went back to the general store where they'd bought peaches three days ago and bought a change of clothes from the skin out… and four more cans of peaches.

They crossed the street to the barber shop; a silver bell jingled when Hunter pushed the door open. The barber came from the back room and said, "Afternoon gents, what can I do for you?"

Hunter said, "I need a haircut, and a shave and a bath in no particular order."

Don said, "I need the same." Hunter turned and examined Dons chin and damned if there weren't a few little whiskers there. Hardly worth the four bits he'd charge him, but what the hell, the man wanted a shave. Hunter got the barber chair first while a kid who worked in the back started hot water for Don's bath.

The barber tried to get Hunter to take a bath in Dons water be shook his head and said, "I got all afternoon for that boy to draw water and I paid my dollar. I'll have a bath that don't have anyone's ass sweat in it." The barber nodded. While Don got his haircut and shave the boy hauled water and brought a cake of soap. Hunter lounged in the hot water long after Don's turn in the barber chair was over. The older he got the better he liked soakin' in a hot tub.

Hunter and Don emerged from the Tonsorial clean and shaved with new clothes. Their old clothes weren't that old; they'd haul 'em back to Texarkana. There was a widow woman there that did Franks wash when he was home. They went to the Sheriff's office. Ed had a paper that Frank and Don had to sign then he gave them a Bank voucher for five hundred dollars. They walked to the Bank and cashed it in. They both refilled their hatbands and had the balance wired to Texarkana. They went to the boarding house and lounged around the parlor downstairs. Hunter read the paper there.There were three newspapers in Terrell. Hunter thought this little town couldn't fill one with news. There was a big story about the new insane asylum they were building. Hunter thought the good townspeople were prob'ly happy about that.

Don went to his room kicked off his boots and took a nap. As far as he knew it was the first afternoon nap of his life. It was fine. He dozed in and out, but even though he'd eaten more for lunch than he'd eaten in the last three days combined, he was hungry again about six in the evening. He pulled the boots back on and went downstairs. Hunter was asleep in the big wingback chair with a newspaper on his lap. Don nudged him and said "I'm goin' to the café. Are you comin?"

Hunter said, "Yeah, I think I will." He got up and walked out. When they got to the café Don ordered roast beef with potatoes, carrots, and cherry pie. Hunter just had cherry pie and coffee. When they were as full as they ever had been they went back and went to bed.

They stopped by the Sheriff's Office on their way out of town in the morning and shook Ed Kilman's hand. When they were riding out Ed handed Frank a sheet of paper. It was a poster. It read, "Dead or Alive One thousand Dollar Reward For Patrick Schultz, Bank Robbery, Cattle Rustling, and Murder. It described him as six foot four inches with blue eyes and sandy blonde hair. 240 pounds. It had a pretty good drawing. The Sheriff said, "If you see this guy bring him to me. I'll make sure the reward comes fast. He's the partner of the guy sittin' in the jail waitin' to swing."

Hunter said, "Ed, I'm stayin' home for a few weeks. I'll wire when I get ready to head out and see if you caught him yet." Ed said, "Fair enough Frank. You boys take care, and I'll see you on the next trip."

They rode away from Mount Pleasant, Texas. They'd be back, several times in the coming years.

They made the usual camp that night and ate the usual rabbit for dinner followed by the usual coffee, along with the peaches which were becoming usual more and more.

29.   Becca

They pulled into Texarkana late the next afternoon. They tied all three horses up at the Three Doors and went inside. Steve was at the bar Hunter said, "Two beers, Steve and use the clean glasses this time." He smiled at Steve.

Steve looked at him and said, "She's not here Frank."

Hunter frowned and said "Where is she?" Steve said, "She's out at your place." Hunter looked puzzled. The place was hoppin' and she was gone?

He asked, "Is she alright; is Liz okay?"

Steve said, "They're fine Frank. She quit, and packed all her stuff in Liz's wagon, and moved it out to your house."

Hunter said, "What happened."

Steve said, "You'll have to ask her about that Frank. I'm swore to silence."

Hunter said, "Well if you won't talk you might as well draw those beers, trail dust still needs washin' out."

Rhonda was already pawin' at Don. She was tellin' him she was so happy to see her fine young gentleman. He was grinning and thinkin' about spending two dollars when the beers came slidin down the bar. Hunter said, "Not tonight Rhonda he's busy tonight."

She said, "Well young man you come back when you have more time." She walked off to help a card player get separated from his money. They drank their beers, and headed out to the house.

Out west of town they rode into the dooryard of a house that seemed it had every lamp lit. They put the three horses in the corral with Liz's two big Morgans. They put a little oats in the trough and made sure the hay was full. Donnie pumped water to fill the trough. Marla came outside at the squeaking of the pump jack.

She said, "Already home? I didn't expect you two for another three days,"

Hunter said, "Dave didn't make it all The way to Decatur. He almost got his brother killed in the bargain."

She said, "Wash the dust off your face in the trough and I'll get your supper started."

Hunter said, "We stopped and saw Steve. He said you quit and moved out here."

She said, "Come in after you've washed and we'll talk."

They washed up and came inside to the smell of pork chops and potatoes frying. There was a rhubarb pie sittin' on the table that still had a couple of big slices left in it. Hunter laid down his saddlebags, and leaned his rifle, and the Greener in the corner closest to the door. Don had left his gear in the barn; that's where he was gonna sleep anyway.

Marla and Liz were moving around the kitchen when Hunter and Don sat down. Marla came to the table and sat down too. She said, "The day you two left something happened here that made me change my life. I have been a saloon girl my whole life, since by bosoms were big enough to hold up a strapless dress. I made no excuses. The money was good and I never wanted for anything. About twenty minutes after you boys left she walked into the Three Doors and I will never do that work again."

Hunter said, "Who walked in?

Marla pointed toward the two little bedrooms and said, "She did. Frank I'd like you to meet your daughter Becca." Hunter turned and looked. It was the same pretty girl who waved and smiled at them from the surrey on their way out of town. Don saw her and smiled she walked to the table and sat down. She said "Daddy, it's a pleasure to finally meet you." Hunter soaked her up with his eyes. She was Marla at nineteen to a tee. Same little nose, same eyes, wild eyes that were blue sometimes but sometimes green with yellow flecks in them. She was beautiful. A fact that was not lost on Don.

Hunter stuck out his hand as if to shake hers and she stood up and hugged his neck. Hunter just said, "I'm glad you're home kid. Are you stayin' long?"

Becca stood up and said, "I live here now Daddy. If it's okay with you." Frank noticed her voice didn't have that nasal Texas drawl that everyone here had. St. Louis had been good for her.

He said, "This is your house. You can live here as long as you like."

Marla said, "We are gonna live here Frank. I quit my job and I know you won't change, so She and I will live here till you come home. Maybe with a family here you'll come home a little more."

Don sat at the table quietly listening to this talk. Almost speechless from Becca's beauty. He couldn't stop staring at her. When Marla said "Donnie this is a two bedroom house I know you have staked a claim to the one on the left."

Don raised his hand as if to stop Marla and said, "Hunter and I have already settled that. I'm moving out."

She said, "You're leaving? Where will you go?"

Don said, "I didn't say I'm leaving, I just said I'm moving out. We're gonna build me a room out at the barn I need my own space when we come back."

Marla smiled, "You men, know what I'm thinkin from a

hundred miles away." Hunter said we were goin' into town for lumber in the morning. If we can borrow Liz's wagon and team that is.

Hunter Said, "By the way Sis, I brought back a little roan mare for you a buggy horse. She ain't much for the saddle but I bet she'd pull a buggy just fine." Hunter looked at Marla and Becca. He said. "I guess we need a buggy too. You ladies can't ride around in a covered wagon all the time."

They had their dinner they talked and laughed. Don went to the barn where his bedroll was still tied to his saddle. He bedded down. The barn was crowded with all of Marla's stuff in there too. Tomorrow He'd stack it all up like they did Liz's. He was tired and happy to be back. He was also excited. He knew Hunter already had another poster. They wouldn't stay long. He fell asleep with those wild eyes Becca had dancing in his head.

Becca and Liz shared the left room and Hunter and Marla shared the right one. She'd brought her big bed from the Three doors and put it in there. They lay down and Frank said in a hushed voice, "Is something wrong with your sister? Don't get me wrong, I am thrilled she's here but I don't understand. Your sister should be like a mother to her. Why would she leave home and come all the way out here to meet some folks she didn't even know?"

Marla said, "I've gotten to know her over the days you were gone. She just walked into the Three Doors like she owned the place and told Steve she was looking for Marla Anderson. He came upstairs and told me a proper young lady was asking for me downstairs and he didn't think she was looking for work. When I came down the stairs I knew who she was without her tellin' me. She told me her name was Becca Hunter and that her Aunt Anna had said her mother was Marla Anderson at the Three Doors Saloon in Texarkana Texas. I told her she was right, and that I am her mother. We talked up in my room all morning about the schools she'd been to and the big city of St. Louis. I told her about going to Dallas and helping Liz move out here was the only time I'd ever been away from Texarkana. Anna never lied to her about us Frank. She knew who and what we were before she came out here. She just feels that we should be together now that she's old enough to deal with it. I walked downstairs about three that afternoon and told Steve I was through, My daughter was home and we were gonna be a family. I gave my keys to Rhonda. She's runnin' the girls there now if Donnie isn't there. I got three cowhands to come out here and get Liz's wagon and they loaded me up and moved me out here. I offered to pay 'em ten dollars each but they wouldn't take it. We've spent the rest of the time getting to know each other, the three of us."

Frank looked her in the eyes and said "I've been tryin' to get you to quit and move out here for years and she got it done in four hours. Well, it don't matter who did it, I'm happy it's done. I have to tell you, I can't stop doing what I do, not yet. Now that you're not workin either what money I make is all we'll have. There is one good thing we won't have to send half of it to St. Louis anymore. Maybe I'll stay home a little more." Marla said "No you won't, so don't even say it. One more thing that really surprised me I forgot to tell you. Anna kept a strict record of the money we sent and what she spent on Becca's needs. When Becca unpacked her bags she handed me an envelope from Anna. In it were those records and twenty two hundred dollars she hadn't spent. It's in your gun cleaning box in the cupboard." Hunter was more than a little surprised.

He said, "Well I guess we'll build Don a house instead of a room since we have all this damned money. In the morning you and I will go looking for a spot."

Marla said, "We'll take Becca too, I saw the way she looked at Donnie. He's taken with her too. She's of marryin' age now too.

Hunter looked at her and said, "Damned women. Got poor ol' Don married at sixteen and he don't even know it yet."

Marla said, "We'll let him know when he needs to know."

The next morning Hunter told Don to get that wagon hitched to those Morgans and we'll go to town for some lumber in a bit. They saddled up Frank's and Don's horses. Frank had Becca on behind him and Marla rode alone. They headed out to the back of the Hunter Farm by the creek. Frank had to spur the big gelding to keep up with her. She seemed to know right where she was going. She got off the paint when she got to the little clearing by the creek. The fields were grown up with brush but once they got to the creek Hunter knew exactly where they were. Marla walked to the center of the clearing and said this is the spot. It's my favorite place on the farm. Hunter knew why. The chances were that Becca was conceived in this clearing right over there by the creek. It was a beautiful spot. The ground was flat enough and the creek never got up in this meadow, even after a big rain. He walked over to the creek and sat down with his back against a tree while the women made their plans.

Hunter thought to himself "Those two are gonna harness Don and put him to work if he ain't careful." He closed his eyes and thought about Patrick Schultz, hidin' out in the territories. Hell he's had time to get to Nebraska by now. Hunter didn't think so thought. They're usually too lazy for that." Hunter thought he was still south of the Canadian River.

The women came over and sat down by Hunter and talked about the front door facing the sunrise and other things. Not thinking about where the barn would someday be. Girls don't think practical. That's when Becca said, "Daddy, why do you hunt outlaws instead of just finding a job somewhere so you could stay home with us."

Hunter thought long and hard before he answered. He didn't want to sound too callous or cold. He was just getting' to know Becca he didn't want her to think him a monster. He started "Becca, I do what I do because it pays well, and that was the only reason at first. Your Mother and I needed to send your Aunt Anna the money it takes to raise a child. I couldn't make that kind of money working for wages. Besides workin' for someone else is like bein' on a six horse stage team, if you ain't the lead horse the scenery never changes. I couldn't see myself spending the rest of my life starin' at a horses ass, still can't. But it became more the longer I did it. This is wild country Becca, there are a lot of wild men out here who don't respect folks. They steal, they kill, they hurt families and the law doesn't have time to track 'em all down. They flee into the Territories and the Texas Sheriffs can't legally go in after them. Don't get me wrong, I don't do it to uphold the law. That couldn't be further from my mind. I do it to hold them accountable for the pain they caused good folks - the kids growin' up orphaned, the farmer who's family won't eat this winter because an outlaw stole the only two cows they had. That's why I do it, and I guess until the law has time to chase 'em and stops printin' the posters I'll keep doin' it.

Becca nodded and said, "Okay, good answer. I'm gonna be here a good long time. I've talked to Momma and you can go as long as you promise to come back every time." Marla smiles at bein' called Momma.

Frank kinda growled, "I do appreciate your permission, but I wasn't asking."

Becca said, "That's alright, I'll let you go anyway." At that she jumped up and said we have lumber to go get don't we. That handsome Donnie is waitin' with the wagon hitched up as we speak.

Hunter said, "I just call him Don. Donnie is a boy's name. He's proved himself a man.

Becca looked at Marla and smiled. Marla said, "We like Donnie better, let's go Frankie." Frank couldn't help but smile. He knew when he was beat and they were gangin' up on him.

27. Stir Crazy

Lumber was bought and hauled. Stones for the foundation were gathered and set. Even Steve came out from the Three Doors and pitched in. Turns out he is a hell of a carpenter. He said, "I left Rhonda runnin' the place. Prob'ly wont be a place left when I get back but I love drivin' nails." Fall was looming on the horizon. Liz was moved into town and School was ready to start in a couple of weeks. She did buy the house that Lowe had rented. She sold the wagon and the Morgans to Frank. He'd have Marla and Becca here to look to the stock now. He'd built a chicken coup, and the hens were layin' pretty regular now.

If they were Lookin' for Becca she'd be down at Don's house helping Don saw boards, or nailing on the batts. She was making herself useful, and keepin' herself in the front of his mind. Her and Don got a calendar and picked a day to be Don's birthday. September the twenty eighth. Becca said that way they could have cake twice in one week. Don wasn't sure even how old she was so Becca decided he was eighteen. It put them a year closer together.

After the Birthdays, Hunter went to town and sent a telegram to Ed Kilman. He sent back that Schultz hadn't been captured but had been seen in the Nations as late as three weeks ago. Hunter wired back that he would leave within the week. He went home and got out his saddlebag and found the poster on Patrick Schultz. The wire he got from Kilman told him the reward was up to fourteen hundred dollars now. They had burned through that money Becca had brought back buildin' that little cottage by the creek not to mention buyin' Liz's wagon and a horse and buggy for Marla and Becca. It was time to go back to work so he could get some rest.

Marla came in the house and Hunter was studying the face on the poster she said, "When ya leavin'?"

He said, "Prob'ly Friday.

She said, "You tell Donnie yet?"

He said, "Not yet. I will tonight."

She said, "You keep him safe Frank Hunter. Your daughter loves that boy, he just doesn't know what to do about it yet."

Hunter said, "I'll keep him as safe as I can.

Friday morning at dawn, in the dooryard of Frank Hunter's childhood home; horses were loaded hugs were given all around and they headed out for the Territories. Schultz had been seen around Fort Reno. It was a long shot, but Hunter believed he would find him there. They always get lazy.

THE END···MAYBE

Made in the USA
San Bernardino, CA
14 July 2017